Piazza
Carignano

ALAIN ELKANN

# *Piazza Carignano*

A NOVEL

*Translated from the Italian
by William Weaver*

The Atlantic Monthly Press
Boston   *New York*

FIRST AMERICAN EDITION

Library of Congress Cataloging-in-Publication Data

Elkann, Alain, 1950–
Piazza carignano.

I. Title.
PQ4865.L485P513   1985   853'.914   86-3532
ISBN 0-87113-109-9

RRD

PRINTED IN THE UNITED STATES OF AMERICA

To my parents

PART ONE

Cinderella

1

I wake up listless, numb. I know I dreamed of unpleasant situations, but I don't remember what. A dim light is filtered through the half-drawn curtain. I grab the alarm: it's seven-thirty. Too early. I could go downstairs and fix the coffee, walk to the corner and buy the newspapers; but the very idea of getting up tires me, and so I fall asleep again.

I feel Cinderella roll over in bed, and she makes funny sounds with her nose. She stretches, gives me a kick; and then, without speaking, she suddenly jumps up, flinging the covers aside with a determined gesture, leaving me half naked.

I don't move. I watch her as she goes into the bath and slams the door. From these first movements of hers I deduce that she's probably in a bad humor. From the bath I hear the sound of objects picked up and thrown on the floor, water pouring down, Cinderella huffing and moaning. Too bad that everything has to be so different after such sweetness! Cinderella comes out of the bath and I'm still in bed; she gives me a hasty glance, doesn't say a word, but heads for the dressing room, where I hear her rummaging around. She puts dresses on, takes them off, tries a pair of slacks, undoes them, and lets them fall to the floor. I am wondering what I have done to her.

She doesn't come back into the bedroom, but goes out another door, and tromps down the stairs. I overcome my dullness, get up, and see through the window the usual grayish weather.

I hear her stirring in the kitchen; she is fixing breakfast, and I wonder whether I should go down in my pareo or get dressed first. Cinderella's wakenings are unpredictable. Some mornings she turns lazily in bed, melancholy, begging in a sweet voice for a cup of tea; on others, seized by pangs of guilt, she washes and dresses and bustles about the house like a fury, emptying ashtrays, plumping up cushions, tearing up envelopes, old newspapers, tidying books and clothes.

I hear a click. On the phone again! Whatever time of day or night it may be, she always has to make a phone call. Sometimes we may be in the same room and she will dart to dial a number and start talking. And, besides that, she will light herself a cigarette and turn her back on me. She talks in whispers as if she were afraid of being overheard.

When she's telephoning it's as if I weren't present; she ignores me even if I make signs to her, asking her to cut it short. She goes right on, unperturbed, in that sweet assumed voice of hers. Sometimes she laughs or is silent for a moment, as if seeking inspiration before she utters her next sentence. It often happens that, in the course of one of her long phone conversations, she will say to the other person, "Hang on a minute; I have to go and get a cracker, because I'm dying of hunger." She will get up, carefully choose a cracker or two, and then, gnawing on one, lazily return to the phone. Most times, in the middle of a sentence, she will say " 'bye" and hang up, ruthlessly.

When the call is over and she sees you there, sitting beside her, she generally smiles: the whole thing seems normal to her, but it can happen that, after granting you that moment of tenderness, she will immediately dial another number. If I ask her with whom she was speaking, she answers as a rule, "A person."

Cinderella doesn't work, but she considers my way of life untidy. She is terribly lazy, but she has to make plans constantly. She has a guilty conscience if she doesn't make a lunch date with someone, if she doesn't have to call on someone else in the afternoon, do some shopping, and in the evening, go to dinner at the house of friends or else to a party.

She rarely asks me to go with her. She insists that she loathes social life because she believes it's a waste of time.

She needs her empty spaces. Almost always she goes out late in the morning, without telling me goodbye, without saying where she's going, and she almost never asks me what my plans are. It's understood that we'll see each other at night, around one or two.

I spend my days in the house, trying to write, and most of the time, as I fail, I kill hours going into the kitchen, fixing a sandwich, drinking a beer, leafing through the papers. Or I watch TV or listen to music. If I feel too lonesome I start phoning friends' houses, where I think I might find Cinderella, and almost always somebody says "She just left" or else "She hasn't arrived yet."

With her it's a matter of pride always to be late. When I can't bear staying in the house any longer, I go out, leaving notes and addresses in case she should come in before I do. Inevitably I wander around a supermarket, where I discover some new kind of canned food, which I end up buying, knowing in advance I'll never eat it; then

I go to a bookshop and am bewildered by the titles and dust jackets and I dream of reading all those books. Then, realizing I don't have much money, after I've picked out several, there comes the moment of choice; I buy one and I'm already yearning for the other ten.

Pleased with my new book, I sit on a bench or go to a pub, where I read the blurb and the first few pages. Then I think of Cinderella and I'm seized by the desire to buy her a dress. I know her sizes well: blouse, medium; shoes, thirty-seven; slacks, forty; dresses, twelve; and pullovers, one size smaller than mine. In my purchases I have to be careful. Buy her one thing at a time, or at most, two things. She appreciates my presents; it amuses her that I clothe her, but she likes few possessions, and those few have to be what pleases her.

But now it's getting late; I'd like to take a bubble bath and wash my hair. Probably the best thing is to ignore her bad humor and wait till she's finished telephoning and had her tea; when she comes up to the bathroom and finds me in the tub, she'll bare her too-white teeth and give me one of those familiar innocent-kitten smiles of hers and ask me what I'm thinking of doing. She'll want to know if we're going to eat out, take a walk, look at an art show; or else she'll tell me we're invited to lunch in the country; or else, with a serious expression, she'll make some comment on a news item she glimpsed in the paper while she was on the phone: some political development or a book review, and she'll adopt a stern, critical tone. She may even come up and, like a butterfly, go into the dressing room, then emerge with a tweed jacket flung over her shoulders, say to me with the same silly smile: " 'Bye, see you tonight."

But if this were one of her hyperactive mornings, in an affectionate impulse or an erotic fit, she would come up with an Oriental lacquer tray, a mug of milky tea, and two slices of whole wheat bread smeared with Oxford marmalade. And we'd end up stretched out, chatting, and we'd make love, spending the day in bed, reading absently, looking at television, everything punctuated, obviously, by countless phone calls.

Since Cinderella is still telephoning, I decide to have my bath, and as I go through the dressing room, I see on the floor one of her aluminum suitcases half packed: two pairs of slacks, two jackets, a book, her diary, and other odds and ends. The suitcase arouses my curiosity, so I wrap a towel around me and rush to the kitchen. I find her with her back to me, sitting on the edge of a chair, speaking into the phone and smoking slowly, undaunted. My presence doesn't ruffle her; I fix my breakfast. I decide to irk her so I make myself coffee instead of herbal tea, I drop in two lumps of white sugar instead of the brown sugar, and I don't take the vitamins that Sebastian brought her from America, which according to Cinderella are fantastic for the heart, the hormones, the skin, and for head colds. I set my cup noisily on the table, I sit down, then I stand up again, and start pacing back and forth in the kitchen, I clear my throat, pick up a cigarette and ask her where the matches are. She turns, smiles at me as if an unexpected guest had arrived, and points to her purse, where there's her lighter.

Furious with myself at this point, because I'm not even capable of making her cut short her phone call, I move into the living room, put on a cassette, *Nabucco,* at top volume, and lie down on the sofa.

I really feel like an idiot; I'm twenty-nine, not ugly, not poor, they say that in spite of my laziness I have a bit of talent, I know plenty of enjoyable and interesting people, and I have to stay here and let myself be treated badly, put up with the ways of a tiresome woman, over thirty-five, not all that beautiful, I don't think, who lives in this gray, decrepit city, having left her husband and children in Paris. If she had at least abandoned them because she's madly in love with me! The truth of the matter is that she wants to be independent, live alone, but she allows her husband to keep her and she calls home every day. I think that in her own way she's in love with me, but she's ashamed of it; she allows me only very small spaces and wants me at all costs to fit into her notion of the boy-lover, to be seen only at home and generally after one o'clock at night. This night-mania of hers is also becoming a drag. We never manage to get to bed before four in the morning, and we can't go to sleep until we've smoked a joint because it's relaxing.

And on the subject of nights, a comical episode occurs to me. It was shortly after we had met and at that time I was living in a little hotel near Hyde Park, patronized mostly by punters on the dog races, Italians, down-at-the-heel Arabs, and provincial Americans. One night Cinderella said she would drop in to say goodbye because she was going to Greece for a couple of weeks. I asked her to spend the evening with me, but she couldn't be persuaded. She said that before seeing me she had to go to dinner where I couldn't accompany her. I made her promise she would come at eleven and I went out to eat with another man, a friend. I came back to the hotel about a quarter to eleven and I told the night clerk I was expecting a lady and would he please send her up.

The night clerk and I had become rather friendly because we were both from Turin and we had made a deal: I lent him money to bet on the dogs and he allowed me to make free phone calls at night, even to the States. I went upstairs and created some disorder in the room, so it would seem more lived in. I decided I would wait for her naked, in bed, drinking whisky. Maybe I would also leave a burnt-out joint in the ashtray. For the musical background I picked out a rock cassette. For a moment I thought it would be more fascinating to stay unwashed and unshaven, but as time went by and she didn't appear, I took a bath. At twelve-thirty, almost resigned to turning out the light and going to sleep, I changed cassettes and put on Lucio Battisti. At quarter to one, I telephoned a friend, and at one-ten I ordered a beer and a sandwich, and finally at one-thirty the night clerk from Turin called to tell me a lady was on her way up.

Weak and in love, I accepted Cinderella's apologies and we spent a few hours together.

When she left, I went with her into the corridor, the door swung shut behind her back, and I was left out there, naked as a jaybird.

The night clerk from Turin came up, pretended not to see me, unlocked the door of my room, and wished me a good night.

Click. At last! I'd like to slap her, leave a pair of marks on her face. It would serve her right: she does nothing but look at herself in the mirror and check the tiniest wrinkle as if it were a dangerous defeat. It's unbelievable, the way no one really knows himself. She is the typical woman who would look well a bit sloppy, tanned, with some wrinkles.

Now she appears at the door of the living room, leaning on the jamb with her idiot smile and her lanky manner. Suede boots look awful on her and I don't understand why, in April, she has to dress for full summer: pink cotton T-shirt, white duck slacks. The slacks are too tight, they make her behind too big, and though she may consider herself the most elegant person on this earth, her white briefs are faintly visible beneath the slacks.

"Did you sleep well? Want a cup of tea?" I hate that indifferent, apathetic way she speaks to me; I'd like to be left alone on my sofa. That's a lie: the truth is that I'd like her to come over to me and give me a kiss.

Sadly, I think of her half-packed suitcase, which means an imminent departure, and I feel alone because I don't know what I'll do with myself in this city, waiting for her to come back.

I hear my voice answer her: "Why did you put on those boots when I've told you a hundred times they look awful on you? I took such trouble to buy you those velvet ballerina slippers at Santini e Dominici, and you've never worn them. I'm sure you don't love me and, even, that you despise me and despise the presents I give you with such love. And another thing. What's the meaning of that suitcase? Where are you going? Why didn't you tell me you were leaving? These mysteries all the time! If you would just once think also about me, the fact that I exist, I breathe, I'm a human being! Now you're going away, and, as always, you won't tell me when you're coming back. Why are you leaving?"

Prolonged, inexpressive smile. She comes into the room, slowly runs a hand through my hair, sits on a strawberry-pink velvet revolving armchair, crossing her legs and slowly transforming the obtuse smile into a watery, perhaps also sad gaze. Without looking me in the face, she says, "I have to leave and you mustn't think it's any fun for me. I didn't tell you because I didn't want to spoil our last evening."

"What does 'last evening' mean?"

"It means we have to stop seeing each other. Philippe

has sued for a divorce. He's going to Mexico to live, and he and I have to discuss the children's future. I don't know yet what will happen. The two boys may go to boarding school, and Lola will come to live here."

"How long have you known?"

"Two days, and I confess I wasn't expecting it. Imagine: a forty-five-year-old man falls in love with a girl, sells everything, abandons everything, and goes to Mexico to become a farmer. I don't even want to think what sort of farmer: a man who's never stuck his nose outside the city, who can't live without telex, office, telephone, secretary, credit cards. Now he's in love and so he's going off to be a pioneer and he wants to take the children with him on the pretext that they'll grow up sturdy and strong. I'm flying to Paris in three hours, to see my lawyer; but first I have to run an errand. In case Lola might come, you'd better clear away your things and go back to live in your studio. I'll call you there if it's possible."

"He falls in love, goes off to Mexico, you become a model mama, and I'm dismissed and told to clear out, 'if possible,' without leaving so much as a grain of dust that might recall my presence."

"Surely you don't think I'll let my children go out there to live? It's not the same as commuting between Paris and London, after all! So I have to get custody, and for that I have to show that I lead a blameless life. I can't abandon my children to such a harebrained father. So you'll just have to be patient. When things have settled down, I'll come to see you, every now and then."

"Excuse me, I don't want to seem vulgar, but in all this business I should stay in my studio like a good boy, waiting for you to show up every now and then! Meanwhile, your husband, tired of the bucolic life, will come back from Mexico and will want to see his offspring again, but Lola will already be of boarding-school age and the boys will be at famous American universities where they'll fall in love with the girl in their English class, and they'll marry and have children, and then the American wife will move from New York to California, to see what it's like to live alone, et cetera, et cetera."

Cinderella is amused, she laughs, moves from the revolving chair and comes over to give me a kiss.

"Forgive me now, but I do have to go. I'll call you from Paris, at the studio."

"What if I wanted to stay one more night?"

"Very well. Of course. But it would be better . . ."

"At least I'll know how to spend the day, but I can't imagine what sort of errand you can run on a Sunday and why — also on a Sunday and so urgently — you have to meet your lawyer."

"I have to buy vitamins for a girl friend in a health-food shop that is always open, and the lawyer is meeting my plane. Divorces and family matters, when they're urgent, can be discussed also on Sunday."

"If I want to call you, where can I find you?"

"They've reserved me a room at the Meurice, but it would be better if you didn't phone. Now I really have to go."

She goes upstairs to finish packing and I remain on the sofa, stretched out, passive.

Basically nothing dramatic has happened, and I start laughing when I think of my move. Today I will go back to my studio, where I have almost never lived.

I'll take a taxi and it will carry me to that neighborhood where I don't know anyone. I'll tidy the place up, buy a few things. I hope they haven't cut off the phone.

This evening I'll read *La Recherche* or *Ulysses*: those are my two favorite books. Favorite objects, rather. For years

I've carried the Pléiade edition of *La Recherche* around with me and a translation of *Ulysses*. I know many stories about the lives of Proust and Joyce, but I've never really read either one of them. This evening I'll start.

Upstairs I hear Cinderella huffing impatiently. The phone rings, she answers, talks for a few moments, and hangs up again.

She closes the case and comes down. I am still lying on the sofa; she is carrying the metal case, a tweed jacket thrown around her shoulders, an Indian silk scarf tied at her throat.

"I asked you please to take off those boots and put on the shoes from Santini e Dominici."

"Do you really think this is the moment?"

"Yes. As you well know: il n'y a pas d'amour sans preuves."

"Do you think a pair of shoes is a proof of love? Can you really be such a baby?"

"The proofs are what someone asks, and for me those shoes have a symbolic value. I was in Rome, on the Corso; I was in a car with four other people, and when in the distance I saw that embroidered red velvet, my heart gave a thud and I imagined you with those shoes on your feet. I let myself be overcome with tenderness, I asked the driver to stop, and I went into Santini e Dominici. When they told me they only had a thirty-seven in black velvet I was desperate. I begged them to look in the warehouse; and, to make a long story short, the next morning they had found a red pair. I couldn't wait to give them to you, I was sure you'd adore them, and I could already see you walking through the streets of London wearing those tender little slippers. When I did give them to you, you barely glanced at them, perhaps you didn't like them and you would no doubt have preferred the black. You wore them

13

just once and I thought you looked stupendous. Now you have to put them on, or else I'll tie you in a chair and won't let you leave, and your extra-special lawyer who even works on Sundays will go to the airport and won't find anyone there."

" 'Bye, make sure you lock up properly, and stick the key under the mat."

She gives me a fleeting kiss and goes off in her boots, without my shoes, gently closing the door.

I look out the window and I see her rummaging in her bag for the car keys; she huffs, becomes nervous, pulls out all the bag's contents, finds the keys, stuffs everything else back into the bag, which she throws, with the suitcase, onto the back seat of the aubergine Fiesta. With a series of jerks, she sets off for the vitamin shop and there's nothing left for me to do but move.

2

Still lying on the sofa, I try to think what belongs to me, what I have left that would be compromising in Cinderella's house. I would like to be one of those people who possess almost nothing, who can pack a suitcase and leave in the space of a few minutes. But unfortunately I am an accumulator of useless things and I am wondering how many suitcases I'll need, to hold books, clothes, objects, cassettes, and other odds and ends.

Finally, ready to go into action, I spring from the sofa like a robot, and with cold cruelty I open drawers, strip shelves, free coat hangers; and the phone rings. It's Cinderella, from the airport.

"Hi, what are you doing?"

"Packing. I think I'll need three taxis. The house is almost empty, and when you come back I advise you to fill it with posters, Babar books, and Beatrix Potter; otherwise Lola might think she has a coldhearted mother."

"Are you going to the studio?"

"Don't worry. I'll be going as soon as I've finished packing."

"I'm calling to ask for the number there; I've lost it."

"If there's no answer it's because they've cut off the phone. In that case, I'll call the Meurice."

"I have to go now; they've announced my flight."

"Do you love me?"

A moment's truce. I imagine eyes staring into the void, liquid; in the crowd, Cinderella, in the too-tight white slacks, has to think in any case for a moment before replying, "Yes," and she adds, with some effort: " 'Bye then; I'll call you."

This unexpected change basically amuses me — going back to my studio after months away from it and thinking that we must officially break up because of force majeure. I'm convinced Cinderella is in love with me, but she's cowardly, weak, lacks the courage to assert herself; she hides. I know very well she has a complex about her father, who died an alcoholic, her insane mother, too much an aesthete and a Catholic, and about having married a rich man, being herself poor with the tastes of a millionaire. But these are things we have talked about too much and today they don't affect me.

I hastily collect my suitcases and sacks in the vestibule, a cardboard box; I am sure I have emptied everything thoroughly and no traces of me are left.

Then I drink a Coke, gnaw on a scrap of cheese, and call a taxi.

The trip in the taxi is like a dream to me. Before leaving I smoked a joint and took a Valium. Now I am sitting back, letting myself be borne along, listening to Vivaldi's concerto for mandolins over the headset.

My apartment is a big studio, with a broad window, the walls lined with bookshelves; the furniture comprises a bed, a sofa, a desk, two straight chairs, and an easy chair. The immediate impression is of a rather cold and dusty

16

place; I leave all my baggage next to the door, rush to the phone, and realize it works. I feel easier; I can stay at home, except for a trip to the supermarket for a few provisions.

I roam around, discovering various objects; I pause to look at old snapshots, I reread some letters, and then, in a burst of energy, I attack the suitcases and take out everything, rapidly putting the clothes in the closets, the books on the shelves. An hour later the studio seems to me in order, inhabitable once more. Now I am finally home, free to do what I want.

Cinderella must have landed. She has no doubt been met by a typical French lawyer who, as I imagine him, looks like a cross between Yves Montand and Lino Ventura, or perhaps he's an older gentleman, a Jean Gabin. I don't know Philippe, but it seems to me he should be a character like Belmondo or Delon. I think how much I dislike French men, too hairy, too talkative, too muscular, always sure of themselves. In France they eat too much meat, too many sauces, they drink enormous quantities of red wine and talk only about politics or vacations. I'd like to call the Meurice, but I wait; I stick to my reading plans. I pick up *Ulysses,* I begin to read. I can't concentrate, and when I reach page eleven I realize it's as if I'd read nothing. I was thinking of Cinderella, who is probably eating with Philippe to discuss the children's future. A husband is always a husband, after all. I slip the bookmark in at page eleven and call the Meurice, where they tell me that madame has arrived but has just gone out.

She'll call me, but it will be at two in the morning.

I lie down on the bed; I look around. My attention is attracted by a little picture of a strip of sand and the sky. I bought it at a flea market in America.

It's been almost three years since I was last in the States, and maybe this would be a good time to take a trip there and write some articles. I could stay at Bob's place. He always says that you have to live either in Milan, because Montale lived there, or on the Upper West Side, between Ninety-first and Ninety-fifth, between Broadway and Riverside Drive. Bob is a poet, a great whisky drinker, a great smoker of Camels without filter; and he always wears sunglasses. After thinking of Bob and after seeing a photograph of New Orleans, I have an irresistible yearning to leave, to go there. I could get a standby flight tomorrow morning: then goodbye to this flabby city, and let Cinderella settle by herself her affairs with the Jean Gabin lawyer and her Belmondo husband.

Now in a good humor thanks to these new American plans, I go to the supermarket and I buy Coca-Cola, beans, and other canned goods. But then I immediately regret having come out; I wouldn't want her to phone just while I'm away from the house. Then I rush back, but since it's only ten-thirty, I decide she can't possibly have telephoned.

I light a candle, a stick of incense, I sit at the desk, and I think of my son, Uguccione, who lives with his mother in Rome, where I see him now and then. Anna never stops nagging me for neglecting the boy, accusing me of being stingy with her alimony; or else she talks to me about her latest loves. Every six months she meets the definitive man in her life and almost always tells me she's decided to change Uguccione's school because the old one isn't right. She tells me that the cause of our wrecked marriage was my instability: she, who since our separation has lived with the child in Berlin, Nice, the Tuscan countryside, Florence, and now Rome. She's a sculptor, she draws, and is a militant feminist. As a result, Uguccione, now nearly seven, has never studied properly, can hardly read, and can't write at all.

I know I'm a terrible father; all I do is send him postcards and take him to Greece for a few days in the summer. I hope that when he's older we'll be able to travel together or go fishing. But it's best for me not to go on too long about this question, which is beyond solution. It seems to me that Cinderella's situation is far more complicated and her dreams of freedom will soon be shattered. At least things between Anna and me are clear; we're divorced and she has custody of Uguccione. Instead of falling back on the past, I have to think of the present. Either I go to Italy to see my mother and Uguccione and meanwhile have a talk with my publisher in Milan, or I leave for the States. To be sure, it's a case of "America the Beautiful," and I feel like a cold, snowy winter, windbreakers, and people skiing in the streets; I want to read the *New York Times* and watch American TV. In Europe I hardly ever watch it, I don't know why not; but there, I'd do nothing else.

The phone rings; it's Cinderella, and from the tone of her voice I sense that things are going badly.

"How are you?"

"Don't ask! Philippe says my behavior is irresponsible, that I've abandoned him, and so he wants to take the children to Mexico with him. He's had his lawyer write a letter accusing me of being mentally incapable and says I would never be able to take proper care of my children. Then he goes on to say that in London I lead a scandalous life with a young boy. How many times did I tell you we had to be more careful? Luckily there's no real proof, and the lawyer says no judge would give my husband custody and allow him to take the children to another continent. But it's going to be a hard fight, and I don't know when or how it'll end. What are you doing?"

"You want me to join you in Paris? I'll stay at the Louisiana and you can come there whenever you're able to."

"Can't you understand? They suspect us, we're probably being followed; the phones are tapped. You have to be seen going out with other girls, foil their suspicions. I won't allow Philippe to take the children from me! I have to hang up now."

"Wait! When will you call me again?"

"I don't know."

"How can I spend my days sitting around the house waiting?"

"If I don't reach you I'll leave a message at Peter's."

"If I want to call you, can't I say I'm an English lawyer? Bruce Glenville, for example?"

"All right, but only if it's urgent. Now I have to go."

Before the click, I hear the sound of a kiss.

After the call, I realize I'm alone and I have to decide what to do with myself. I could go to New York and stay at Bob's, but I could also join the Foreign Legion or visit China, go to Colombia for a fabulous high, or to see Roberto in Brazil. And instead I'm here, tomorrow is Monday and I'll be waked up by Leonarda, my part-time cleaning woman from Salerno, who pretends to do the studio. She cheats on the number of hours and I know it. Instead of working she drinks coffee, chatters, and listens to the radio. Maybe tonight I'd need to confide in my bosom buddy or my mama, but I'm alone with Joyce, whom I don't feel like reading, so I think the wisest thing is to take another Valium and try to sleep, expecting tomorrow morning a noise at the door, and then: "You dormite qui senza let me know. I don't comprare milko. You solo? Or I make two caffè?"

This is Leonarda's language, half and half.

PART TWO

Turin

3

I soon had to give up my dreams of alternative lives, because something unforeseen happened, and all is changed.

My mother is seriously ill and I have been urgently
summoned to her bedside. I am virtually trapped in an old
family villa twenty kilometers from Turin, in the role of
son, housekeeper, and superintendent. I have to talk with
the doctors, give instructions to the nurses, and begin to
understand the entangled affairs of the family.

Cinderella is still in Paris, and I talk with her from time
to time, using the fake name Bruce Glenville.

Since my arrival here, I have spent a large part of my
time trying to fend off the various aunts, the numerous
cousins, and a whole array of friends who do nothing but
telephone for news or suggest other doctors or different
cures. One aunt insists that our present doctor is extraordinary; another aunt says he is terrible and will kill my
mother. One says the day nurse steals, and the other wants
to take over at night to save money.

And so I spend my days in a large group of relatives,
most of them strangers to me; and I have the sensation
that I am living a posthumous childhood. My mother knows
nothing of all this turmoil: she's too ill. I see her for five

minutes every two days, often in the presence of a nurse and the doctor. Our relationship is confined to exchanged glances, a light pat, silences, murmured words. It is difficult for me to ask myself: "Do I love my mother?" It is an obvious love, and for this very reason difficult to define. Am I here out of a sense of duty, or for love? I don't know, but I don't feel I could be anywhere else. Sometimes I think my presence here is useless. Although I'm her only son, I'm only one person among many who have a claim to a piece of my mother. Now and then, whether it's jealousy or self-importance, I want all the others to disappear; I want to be the only one in charge, the one responsible. There are moments when I wish she would die quickly, so I wouldn't have to watch her suffer. I sometimes imagine they will come and wake me in the night to announce her death.

Then still more relatives will arrive, and the rabbi will perform the religious rites. From all sides flowers will come and telegrams of condolence, and friends will volunteer for the wake. There will be a family council to prepare the obituary for the newspapers and then the tiny, dead body will be entrusted to the various employees of an undertaker's firm, who will take charge of organizing the funeral down to the smallest detail.

Once she is buried, after a sad family meal, the notaries and lawyers will take over, and there will be the reading of the will.

It would be best if she died in August; the city is virtually deserted, the ceremony would be simpler, and she would suffer the cold less. But if she were to die during the mid-August holiday, it would be impossible to bury her at all.

When I think that she can die at any moment, I stay in the country; if I imagine it will be a matter of months,

24

then I sometimes decide to go into Turin. But if it seems a death-agony destined to last for years, then I feel remorse at my neglect of Cinderella and I tell myself I should give her a surprise and slip up to Paris for a few days.

I miss her presence; I miss her faults, and our habits.

I'm sure that the knowledge of my being here in this remote countryside, surrounded by relatives, reassures her of my fidelity. Unfortunately our phone conversations are very brief; the aunts buzz around the phone and tell me to hurry up because we are inexorably awaiting a call from the doctor. Reminding me of my early childhood in Turin, my aunts keep urging me to get in touch with so-and-so who is now an accountant or with someone else: married, an engineer at Fiat who always asks after me and would be so happy to see me again! I prefer to see no one; I cherish my solitude, and I also avoid the dinner invitations of certain cousins when they come to see my mother.

At meals I sit at the head of the table, in my grandfather's place. This is the decision of Lucia, an elderly maid, who has appointed me head of the family, now that my grandfather is dead. The old family customs are still maintained: dinner at quarter to one and supper at quarter to eight.

My favorite aunt is Miriam Löwenthal, who is usually in Paris; an aunt who actually is a cousin and has long been my mother's best friend. She and I talk always of the past and exchange family stories: about her father, her mother, and about how attached her mother was to a brother, Uncle Tullio, who was a big Fascist. I had heard about Uncle Tullio also from my grandfather, who described him as a man of great refinement, an excellent musician and first-rate writer. The Fascist aspect was played down because, after the war, with the creation of the state of Israel, the Treves family all became Zionists and anti-

Fascists, and always referred to "that pig Mussolini" and to Tullio as "poor Tullio." My Löwenthal aunt told me that I would find some of Uncle Tullio's books in the library and that it might amuse me to read some pages.

I decided to read those books and I started looking for them, convinced I would find treatises on the Fascist mystique. Instead I found a tract against Zionism, a collection of verses, and a personal interpretation, written in 1935, of the events concerning Caporetto and Vittorio Veneto. Everything is in D'Annunzian style, the Duce is omnipresent, praised to the skies in every instance. With great vehemence Uncle Tullio acclaims the valor of the Italian soldier at the front. In his books Uncle Tullio, who won Fascist literary awards, belonged to Mussolini's first paramilitary squads, and was an ardent nationalist, also emerges as a militarist, conservative, monarchist, and throughout everything there is a hint of madness, but also of something rather frivolous.

As I stay here, I discover a Turin I didn't know as a child, and it has become my village. The embankments, piazza Vittorio, via Po. After I have strolled for a bit, I may sit for a while at the Bar Elena, a little café with marble tables. The bartender is like something out of a child's comic strip. Tall and thin, slightly bent, with thick mustache and pince-nez. The bar's customers are all kids, and sometimes I feel a desire to go and live in that square. I feel I would write crime novels there or draw caricatures.

There has been a new turn of events in our rural life: Aunt Elvira has quarreled with Aunt Miriam on the subject of Uncle Tullio, and with the pretext that there are too many people in the house, Aunt Miriam has decided to move to the Pensione Europa, in piazza Castello.

The reason behind the quarrel is that Aunt Elvira was

trying to make light of the fact that Uncle Tullio was a Fascist, whereas Aunt Miriam said he had been the real thing, with great sincerity, and that her parents, though they had always been socialists, respected him and considered him an honorable man.

4

I enjoy calling on Aunt Miriam at the Pensione Europa because, as both of us have lived almost all our lives in foreign countries, we have many tastes in common.

At the villa, my various relatives from Turin and Milan have taken charge. But apart from vague, teary remarks about my mother, all they do is repeat local gossip or speculate about the will. I know I am a great source of irritation for them, because as an only child, I am my mother's sole heir. My prospects as a future man of wealth and Aunt Miriam's reputation as a billionaire constantly provoke contemptuous little jabs of envy. Understanding perfectly the way things stand, Aunt Miriam and I have decided to transfer our friendly, natural sessions to the Pensione Europa.

And coming out with me amuses her, and also gives her an excuse to change, to dress up. Aunt Miriam is very tall, with long reddish hair, which she gathers in a chignon. She is sturdily built; she could be anywhere between sixty-two and sixty-eight. She always wears thick eyeglasses with an amber frame and dark blue lenses. One eye is sightless, but she won't wear a monocle because she considers it antidemocratic.

As a rule she wears Chanel suits, carries a crocodile handbag, a big sapphire on her finger. She smokes slowly, Chesterfields, with or without holder. Her French is very mannered and fashionable, and she enjoys occasionally affecting an English accent. Like me, she reads the *Herald-Tribune* and finds Italian papers unreadable, except for the illustrated weeklies. We talk often about trips we've taken, about books, music, politics. I listen with curiosity when she tells me about her life in Paris before the war, the visits to Turin to my grandparents' house. It seems that the Treves family always called her father simply "Löwenthal," with a mixture of envy and contempt. Contempt because he wasn't a nobleman, hadn't been an officer, was a socialist, and in Paris spent his time with a number of anti-Fascist Italians. Envy because he was very rich, a friend of Léon Blum, senator, banker, expert in monetary questions, and a well-known collector of art objects. Aunt Miriam becomes radiant when she speaks of her father: "Il était beau, grand, des énormes yeux bleus qui faisaient peur à tout le monde, mais avec moi et je dois dire même avec maman, il était d'une tendresse spéciale. Il avait des mains sublimes; le seul homme que j'eusse connu qui puisse porter une chevalière de cette importance!" she said, holding up her sapphire.

We always end up talking about Uncle Tullio, because he was particularly attached to Miriam's mother and it seems he went often to Paris. He went there for work or to meet groups of French Fascists, but he never failed to pay a visit to the Louvre. He was interested in the paintings of Poussin, Claude Lorrain, but he had a supreme passion for the Winged Victory of Samothrace and for two pictures of Delacroix, *Les Femmes d'Algers* and *La Mort de Sardanapale*. Miriam remembered that her uncle refused to be a guest in their home and preferred a hotel on boulevard

Raspail, the Lutetia, which later became the SS headquarters.

Miriam remembered her uncle Tullio, short, fat, with a pink face, and blond, curly hair.

One morning I arrived at the Pensione Europa early and they asked me to wait in the corridor: a long corridor, broad and dark, with a floor of ugly patches of marble and a threadbare strip of carpet. I sat down, and I saw a girl standing and telephoning, at a pay telephone, whose plastic shield hid her face.

She seemed very young, tiny; I was impressed by her features and her elegance. I noticed her also because she was only a few paces from me and she spoke in a hoarse voice, with an unpleasant, authoritarian tone, imparting orders, huffing, using stern words, but always maintaining her calm.

She smoked a great deal and I could see clouds of smoke that kept coming from that half-booth.

When she put out a cigarette, I saw that she had small hands, beautiful, slender, veined, tanned, and she wore two rings, one on her little finger and one on her index finger.

After yet another impatient huff, I heard the click, then more tokens and another call. I thought of Cinderella, as the girl telephoned, still smoking, her elbows propped on the glass shelf beneath the phone, unaware that she was being observed. She swayed her minuscule behind and spoke, this time, almost in a whisper. It seemed incredible to me. I looked again: she was wearing embroidered red shoes from Santini e Dominici. I felt a thud in my heart. I was afraid that the call wouldn't end and Aunt Miriam would arrive. Suddenly I felt terribly bored with stories of before the war and if the face of the girl phoning and smoking was the way I imagined it, I would have liked to ask her to come out to the Bar Elena or to a trattoria, then to go to the embankment, to a bookshop, to buy some records. With that girl I would have liked a room in some modern hotel: music, bar, air-conditioning, light switches, no dust, no old rugs but wall-to-wall carpeting, grass green or red. Click. She put out the cigarette, then she turned.

Dark blond hair, not very long, slightly waving; a narrow little nose, freckles; huge blue eyes, thick brows; a tiny, nervous body.

She didn't see me and began to walk, pensively, up and down the corridor, her arms folded, almost twisted, behind her back, her head high. She was looking up, into the void, she could have tripped; she was walking slowly, with one foot turned out. But I saw that, after the first few steps, she pulled that foot in, with an effort. I couldn't tell if it was an unusual way of walking or if she had such grave thoughts that she was unaware of that tic.

A door opened and, wearing a dark strawberry Chanel suit and blue glasses, Aunt Miriam came toward me. She greeted me affectionately, and seeing the girl approach, she stopped her, gave her a slap on the shoulder, and said to her: "I see you're following my advice and doing your exercises. Good, good. Don't forget: six times a day, every day, and at night the pillow. Haven't you met? This is my cousin, and this is Thüsis." We said hello shyly, shaking hands, and I felt that she had peaceful hands, gentle but bony. I thought Thüsis was perhaps a nickname. My aunt went on, "How stupid of me not to have introduced you before: these memory lapses of mine are becoming dangerous; I must talk about them with Morvan the moment I get back to Paris. In this uncivilized town I'm sure there isn't a doctor who can treat amnesia. Well, will you come and lunch with us?" While Aunt Miriam talked, the two of us looked at each other with complicity.

"No, thank you, Madame Löwenthal; I have a lesson today, so I can't. Thank you."

She spoke in a voice different from her telephone voice. I was disappointed; when would we meet again?

"I can't understand you, my child. You cry on my shoulder and tell me about your terrible loneliness, I introduce you to a divine boy, and you run away! We'll catch you all the same; in fact, as soon as there's a sunny day we'll take you to the villa for a picnic, just to spite that bunch out there! You're too pale, dear, you need to get some air. Ballet's not the only thing in this world."

Thüsis whispered a timid "Au revoir."

Leaving her, I felt my heart pounding; my legs seemed hollow. Now I would torment my aunt with questions, but I was sure that she would talk to me about entirely different things, according to her rule that "la jeunesse doit apprendre l'art de la patience."

5

"Of course, you fell in love at first sight! That Thüsis really is a special girl! I don't know how to say it: though she's not Jewish, she has a certain juiverie. You know what I mean? Her mother's an alcoholic, lives in the States; they never see each other. Her father died of a heart attack; he was the only person who counted, in her life. Now her uncle Bill, her father's brother, acts as her guardian. Thüsis has come to Turin to take ballet lessons from a Russian teacher, some woman named Tanya, who is supposed to be wonderful. They say she danced with Nijinsky, but I find that hard to believe."

"You met Thüsis at the Europa?"

"Yes. You've probably noticed she has a strange way of walking."

"No."

"Well, she does. I gave her some suggestions about how to correct the problem. Then, you know how it goes, we started talking, and pretty much exchanged our life stories. It's always enjoyable to have young women friends."

"Do you think I'll see her again? I have the feeling she took a dislike to me."

"Why, what are you saying, mon cousin? I'll arrange for you two to meet. A pair of lonely hearts . . ."

I thought it wasn't a good idea to have yourself introduced to a girl by your aunt. I wanted to try to meet Thüsis without any help. Obviously, that isn't how it worked out, because Aunt Miriam didn't give me time to think. She immediately invited me to the Pensione Europa the next day.

She received us in her sitting room and then apologized, saying that she wasn't feeling very well. Thüsis and I went out by ourselves, both a bit shy. She spoke very little and smoked constantly. I asked her, "Are you bored?"

"No."

"What are you doing in Turin?"

"I'm studying dance with Tanya. She's a wonderful teacher. Besides, dance and magic go together. Turin is magic, it's melancholy. I feel nobody can touch me here; and the mountains are close, too."

"Would you like to come and see me in the country?"

"I don't know. What did you say your name is?"

"Alberto Claudio. I'm a writer. Usually, I live in London, but I came out to take care of my mother, who's very ill. She lives in the country, near Turin. I'm an only child. My father was a Resistance hero. He died when I was three. I grew up with my mother. Then in boarding school, and then I traveled, and studied. What about you?"

"Is your mother beautiful?"

"Yes, very."

"My mother's an alcoholic. I was brought up by my father. I used to call him Daffy; he died of a heart attack two years ago. Thüsis is the name of a little village in Switzerland. He called me that because to him it seemed a name that worked for male and female, and since he

34

wanted a son, he treated me like a boy and he called me Thüsis. My mother never bothered about me. In his own way, he taught me everything. Anyway, if your mother's very ill, it doesn't sound like a good idea for me to come and see you in the country."

"Is there a man in your life?"

"Is there a woman in your life?"

"I'm not sure."

"I don't think about it; I dance. I was in love with a Greek boy who's studying in Boston; but I think I'll never be able to find a man like my father."

"I love, or thought I loved, Cinderella, an Englishwoman, older than me; but it's impossible. She has to think about her children. Forgive me if I seem abrupt, and maybe this isn't the right way to say it, but I'd like to stay with you. I think I've fallen in love with you, and I wouldn't want to lose you."

"It takes two to be together. You're sweet, but I can't do it. You have another person, and it all seems too hurried to me."

"I know I've loved you since the first moment I saw you, at the pension. I'd like us to be together, here in Turin, while we're here, in transit."

"Now we'll eat and then go out . . ."

We quickly left the restaurant and went back to the Pensione Europa.

From an untidy drawer full of junk, Thüsis produced some pornographic magazines and made me leaf through them, as she began masturbating, undressing, then giving me her body as if it were merchandise to be handled. As I made love I told her I was attracted only by older women because their breasts are flabbier.

"I only like effeminate men. I wish you'd put on lipstick and nylon stockings and paint your fingernails red."

During those hours that we lay naked on the bed, she let the same record keep playing over and over. A tango, the volume very low. When we were finally exhausted, she asked me: "Shall we call Aunt Miriam in, too? Maybe being with us would give her a kick, too. You would touch her breasts, which are bound to be flabby."

The girl I had invited to lunch had a way of behaving in bed that made Cinderella seem like a schoolgirl. When dawn was beginning to break, she said to me in a hoarse voice: "This will sound absurd to you, but tonight I fell in love with you. I wouldn't have thought we were so alike!"

"Neither would I," I replied, banally, and then we fell asleep, hand in hand. I woke to find the bed empty and a note: "I'll wait for you at Tanya's school: via Po, 14. Lessons end at six. I love you. Thüsis."

I felt some shame, thinking of my mother and the way I had vanished. And what if I ran into Aunt Miriam? Luckily I left the Pensione Europa unseen.

As soon as I reached the villa, Aunt Elvira told me that Miriam was coming to lunch, and Mama had asked for me, and then, in a tone of mounting reproach, she added: "I don't know who that person with the foreign accent is, who keeps calling you; but you must tell her that this is a respectable household and it isn't proper to call after nine in the evening."

"Did she say where she was?"

"She asked you to call her at home."

Cinderella had gone back to London!

"At last!"

"I was out."

"Are you coming to London?"

"Yes, but I don't know when. I have to stay with my mother."

There was one of the usual silences, then she said: "Now there's a person here. I'll call you later."

"No, better not. If you're staying there a few days, I'll call you."

"Don't leave messages. Call me tonight."

"I may not be able to."

" 'Bye." I heard the smack of a kiss.

I thought how cruel living is.

She was implacable in her certitude, in her hanging up the telephone, but she hadn't given me the time to tell her that perhaps she had lost me, that in the night, in a Turin pension, I had known an incredible, stupendous woman, and I had fallen in love with her.

After lunch I went off with Aunt Miriam and told her I loved Thüsis.

"I knew, and it seems an excellent thing to me; you should invite her here. She could have my room!"

"What about the other relatives?"

"It will be good for them to get used to the idea that this is your house. I know you'll marry Thüsis, and I'd like you to introduce her to your mother."

"But doesn't it seem a bit premature to you?"

"I'll come to supper with her tomorrow evening. I'll say she's a niece of mine from America."

6

At the Bar Elena, Thüsis talked to me about Daffy: "The last years he lived almost all the time on Corsica. He had an estate near Ajaccio. He ran the farm, he painted, or else he went out in his sailboat. On the boat he treated me like a cabin boy and on the farm like a peasant. He almost never asked me questions, he called me 'la petite américaine,' because I lived in the States. Together, we spoke in Corsican dialect, English, French, all mixed up. I spent my vacations with him. Now his brother, Uncle Bill, manages everything. He's a very different man from my father, and I don't have a good relationship with him. Daffy had blue eyes, like a lunatic, like an angel. He didn't say much, and if you didn't know him well, since he was a grouch and had a deep voice, he could inspire fear. My mother left because she couldn't live with a man who never said anything and was very simple and led a lonely life. When he went to New York, usually between October and Christmas, he behaved like a man of the world, but he got bored soon and came back to the country. He died of a heart attack. They also say he was murdered by a bandit: a question of honor. As far as I know he was found dead in his hotel room. At least that's what my uncle and my mother told me. The papers didn't say anything about it; I was in boarding school in Virginia. Daffy listened to lots of classical music, danced the tango marvelously; he lived for several years in Buenos Aires after the war, before he got married. There was a Spanish side to him. I remember that sometimes he would take me to see the corrida, in Nîmes."

Thüsis spoke with mounting excitement: "You see, he was a volunteer in the Spanish war and then in World War Two. He wore dark clothes, had white hair, smooth, always neatly combed. He was used to living in the open, in the sun, his skin was tan, he had harsh, rather sharp features. I don't think he was very tall. They say that he sometimes became violently angry and that he was fiercely cruel. This is what my mother always says; and half the time she accuses him of having been homosexual and the rest of the time she says he was unfaithful to her with many other women. But that's enough! I don't think I've ever talked this much about him. Forgive me, but I feel I'm falling in love with you and it's as if I had to tell you that, before, he was there. Don't be frightened."

"No, I'm fascinated."

Thüsis didn't want us to spend the night together; she said she would come to supper with Aunt Miriam.

Going back to the villa, still caught up in that story of Daffy, I found a chill message from Aunt Elvira: "For the last time I must ask you to tell that *lady* to telephone at civilized hours!"

I called Cinderella, but she was out. A moment later Anna called me, to explain that Uguccione would have to change schools, because it would be much better for him to go to a private institution. And furthermore, if he went to an English or a French school, he would become bilingual. Obviously the question of money arose. I could give her more, make an effort. The child support I was giving her for Uguccione at this point didn't even cover medical expenses . . . I had to break off the conversation because my mother had taken a turn and we had to call the doctor. I had barely hung up when Aunt Elvira, in an irritated tone, told me that the "lady" was on the phone and could I please make it brief.

"I called you last night, but you didn't answer."

"I was out."

"How are things going?"

"I have to go back to Paris. Everything is always more complicated than you think it'll be. How's your mother?"

"She's very bad, and unfortunately it's always impossible to talk in this house! Maybe it would be best for us to call it all off. I think I've met a girl."

"What's she like?"

"Very beautiful, with crazy erotic tastes, very complicated family history. She smokes all the time; she's a dancer. I don't know much about her, I've just met her."

"Are you in love?"

"I think so."

Cinderella hung up. I shouldn't have told her in that way!

Living seemed to me a terrible misunderstanding. An irrevocable series of events, linked and inconclusive, all connected with me. How I longed to be left alone, to know Thüsis better!

The doctor arrived; the examination was long, thorough.

Coming out of my mother's room, he said: "I can't make a precise diagnosis. She must be kept under careful observation, and she mustn't be disturbed. Rest. Plenty of rest. . . . It could be just a flare-up."

✳ ✳ ✳

40

The supper with Thüsis and Aunt Miriam at the villa was memorable. My relatives, and especially Aunt Elvira, assumed a pompous tone, which they all considered proper to the situation, conveying the idea that "in view of my mother's condition, it was profoundly immoral and improper for me to invite an outsider to supper."

As if she meant to punish the others, Aunt Miriam started acting out a little play with Thüsis, whom she introduced as an American niece, in Turin to study Egyptology. Aunt Miriam told the others to be nice to the girl because her mother was someone very dear to my mother, and since the unpleasant atmosphere at the villa had obliged Miriam to go and live at the Pensione Europa, this niece, whenever she wished, could come and stay in Miriam's room, "which had been poor Tullio's, as a boy."

7

Someone at the Bar Elena suggested we rent an attic studio in piazza Carignano. It was a big room under the eaves, unfurnished, fairly clean, with a tiny kitchen and bath. We fell in love with it at first sight, took it immediately, and fitted it out with some makeshift furniture we bought at a flea market.

Unfortunately my mother's serious condition didn't enable me to settle there, and I had to go back and sleep at the villa. Since it was very hot in Turin, I seized the opportunity to invite Thüsis out, to stay for a few days in Uncle Tullio's room, as Aunt Miriam had suggested.

This, however, turned out to be a very bad idea. The constant phone calls from Cinderella and Anna made Thüsis nervous. And further, both my relatives and the staff did nothing but complain of our scandalous conduct: our scuttling back and forth in the night, Thüsis's way of going into the kitchen to make herself a sandwich at the most unlikely hours, and the fact that she never screwed the top back on the jar of mayonnaise or jam, and at table she never finished what was on her plate. For the first few days Thüsis seemed to pay little attention to these tiny reproaches, and she looked on everything as if it were an amusing joke, but then an unforeseen rebellion exploded in her.

One evening, when Aunt Miriam came to supper, Thüsis began by saying, "In this house they do everything they can to make our life impossible, and Alberto Claudio is incapable of defending himself: he hasn't any character. Besides, it's no use saying I'm your niece if a thirty-year-old man can't have a woman respected in his own house. If they were going to complain so much about our movements in the night, all they had to do was not put us in separate bedrooms. If my mother and his really were friends, don't you think it would have been polite to suggest I pay a visit to Alberto Claudio's mother, seeing that I've been in her house for four days?"

After that unexpected outburst, everyone seemed outraged, and even Aunt Miriam was embarrassed. I kept quiet, and the moment supper was over, Thüsis went off and shut herself up in her room, which she then didn't leave for almost two days. I tried in vain, and on countless pretexts, to persuade her to come out, but it was hopeless. So I lived between my anxiety at that silence and the upbraidings or ironic smiles of my relatives. It was a situation from which, in any case, I couldn't escape, as my mother's health was worsening.

I kept slipping little notes and letters under Thüsis's door, which she disdained, not even picking them up. I begged her to forgive me, but she showed me no sign of life; and the others were all laughing at me. They said to me that, after all, this was my house, and if she chose to behave like this I should order her to clear out.

After two days' confinement, Thüsis appeared in my bedroom in the middle of the night. She slipped into bed, and muttered to me: "Coward! Make love to me this minute or I'll yell and wake the whole house and your mother will die of heart failure."

As soon as we finished making love, she left my room, and I followed her toward hers, but she promptly locked herself in, saying: "Don't bother me or I'll scream."

I could have made some spectacular gesture, like kicking down the door and forcing my way in, but her grumpy attitude piqued me. There were moments when I was worried; I convinced myself that I was desperately in love with a mentally unbalanced girl who was hurting me, but then I reassured myself, convinced now that this was a way of hers, trying to seduce me and attract attention. A nascent love has to be exclusive.

I became the object of constant hints. Thüsis's place at table was always laid, and deserted. Uncle Gustavo turned to Aunt Elvira and asked: "Do you think we can start dinner, or must we wait for our guest?"

"We'll wait another moment, in case the girl decides to put in an appearance. She might take offense, and it would be a shame to seem rude, to a person with such perfect manners."

At lunchtime, just as Uncle Gustavo was asking whether or not we should wait for Thüsis, she appeared, elegantly dressed, her face made up, provoking.

She had the eyes of a purring cat, and she spoke to all of us with great propriety, as if nothing had happened. She promptly inquired about my mother's condition and said to Aunt Elvira, "I would be so happy if I could say goodbye and thank Alberto Claudio's mother, who has so kindly had me as her guest, unawares; because tomorrow morning I must leave."

Aunt Elvira replied that it would be possible for her to speak with my mother in the late afternoon. I asked Thüsis if she and I could talk, but she said she had nothing to say to me. I tried to draw her into a corner of the garden, away from the alert ears of the inhabitants of the villa, but there was nothing doing.

She went to meet and thank my mother, and then shut herself in her room again and didn't come down for supper.

I walked back and forth under her window, which remained illuminated all night, as if she were saying: "I protest and I won't sleep."

To avenge myself, I called Cinderella; it was almost four, but she wasn't in.

The next morning I was still asleep when Thüsis, coming into my room, said: "Get dressed and take me to the bus stop."

"I'll take you to piazza Carignano."

"I'm going back to the Pensione Europa, but I'm taking the bus."

"Listen, this whole business is absurd; it can't go on. What's happening with you? You could at least tell me you don't want me anymore. May I ask what I've done to you?"

"I'd like you to make up your mind whether you're in love with me or with that ghost you're always talking to on the phone."

"What's that got to do with anything?"

"When you've decided who you're in love with, we can see each other again. I have to go now. Hurry up."

She was very thin, tall, and she seemed younger as she ran toward the bus, a yellow nylon bag slung over her shoulder.

So I sat at a café in the village square, opposite the town hall. I drank some juice, ate a brioche, and thought how strange this period was. There was nothing left of what had been my life for a long time: no contact with my publisher, my house in London abandoned, and also my books, my friends.

I was bound to London only by those boring, nighttime phone calls; otherwise I lived among alien people, my mother's death-agony, and a love.

Was Thüsis the woman of my life? Certainly she attracted me very much.

I felt a moment of unusual peace in that village square, still half asleep and cool, where the first rays of the sun were just beginning to make themselves felt.

I don't know why I hurried back to the villa and rushed into Thüsis's room.

There was a horrible smell of smoke; otherwise it was in perfect order, the bed made; and my letters had vanished. Swallowed up by the yellow bag.

So she did love me a little.

I called her at the Pensione Europa, and they told me she had gone out. I tried again, and they answered that she had given instructions not to be disturbed. I tried to persuade the operator, but to no avail. Then I decided to go into the city and send flowers. As I was leaving, Aunt Elvira said to me: "That girl is no good. Thank heaven she's left. In her room they found overflowing ashtrays, empty cigarette packages, and a bottle of whisky under the bed. Shameful!"

8

I turned up at the Pensione Europa with a bunch of pink roses. I asked a maid to give them to Thüsis from me, and to ask if she had anything to say to me. The maid came back, carrying the roses, and said: "The signorina asked me to remind you that her favorite flowers are cornflowers, and she didn't think it very appropriate to be given flowers with thorns."

Humiliated by my mistaken choice, I tried all the florists of Turin in search of cornflowers, but I didn't find any. So I bought some daisies and wrote a little card to Thüsis: "Unfortunately I couldn't find any cornflowers, so I chose the simplest flowers I could find."

This time the maid came back with a note for me.

"Dear Alberto Claudio, maybe it would be best for you to decide whether or not you want to go on with your London phone calls. If you should consider them no longer necessary, I'd suggest you drop by piazza Carignano and water the plants; and if you should go back and live there, maybe buy yourself a fan. I'll have to come and talk to you soon. Yours, Thüsis."

Despite the sarcasm, this was a message of peace. Thüsis was jealous, and she couldn't bear taking second place. I arranged things so that I could go back to live in piazza Carignano: I bought a fan and I'll see my mother when it's my turn to be with her. I have worked out a system so they can get in touch in case I have to rush there in an emergency.

While waiting for Thüsis, I wrote to my grandfather Dimitri, as I had been planning to do for days. I'd like him to come to Turin and see my mother before it's too late. My grandfather Dimitri is the only survivor on my father's side of the family; he's ninety-two and he looks seventy. Born in St. Petersburg in one of those families Tolstoy described so accurately, he's been living in Paris since 1917; sculptor, violinist, philosopher, collector. He looks like a prewar ambassador: he's the most elegant man I've ever seen, always wearing a blue suit, loose silk shirts, and precious cuff links of onyx and diamonds.

When I think of him, I see him walking in the cold Paris winter, bundled into a great dark overcoat, of bristling fur, with a slightly floppy black hat; he leans just a bit on a cane with a lapis lazuli handle. I'd like to grow old, too, in order to have a white, wispy beard like his, and those fleshless, veined hands covered with dark freckles. On his left little finger he wears an opaque emerald, square cut; and as he speaks, he accompanies his words with light and perfect gestures. Even though it will be a great blow for him to learn that my mother is gravely ill, he will at least have the consolation of not having learned it too late.

9

In piazza Carignano this afternoon a maid from the Pensione Europa turned up, carrying with some difficulty an old-fashioned gramophone and a pile of 78s. She begged my pardon for barging in, but signorina Thüsis had asked her to deliver these things and had also given her a list of objects that had to be moved into the kitchen. I pretended to know all about it, and I allowed the maid to work undisturbed, carrying into the kitchen the tape player, the radio, the alarm clock, the night lamp, and other objects. She shifted the potted palm and the rare ficus that Thüsis insisted I keep watered; she also removed the counterpane and replaced the salmon-colored sheets we had bought at the Rinascente with white sheets and a worn blanket. After she had transformed the studio, giving it a gloomy, old-fashioned atmosphere, the maid held out the gramophone and asked me if I could put on the Wagner record the signorina had chosen since she would be arriving any moment. The signorina had also asked her to tell me that she would like to find me lying on the bed in a light silk robe reading a book by Evola. A final instruction: I was to get rid of the fan and keep the windows wide open. When the maid finally left, I decided to obey Thüsis's instructions to the letter, without asking why.

Almost immediately she arrived, wrapped in a dark fur down to her feet, dressed like a middle European woman of the 1930s, with a little hat and veil, long suede gloves, stockings with seams; and she was heavily made up and powdered. She entered, smoking a cigarette in a long tortoiseshell holder, steeped in a somewhat opiate perfume. She was holding two bottles of champagne. After the maid's orders and since I wanted to make peace, I waited for her to speak first.

"I don't want you to ask me questions, I want you to allow yourself to be called just Claudio, and not be insulted by what I say to you, and instead of thinking about what happens and why it happens, just let yourself go. The only important thing is for you to transfer yourself mentally into the following situation: we are in piazza Carignano, it is December 1943, and freezing, half the windowpanes are broken. I am your mistress, and I arrive here with two bottles of champagne bought on the black market. You're listening to Wagner, lazy and fatalistic, and you're waiting for me, eager for sex and lust. Remember, too, that after a certain moment the bombing begins and while all the other tenants go down fearfully to the shelter, you and I stay in bed, extracting the maximum pleasure from our deliberate, dangerous recklessness. Is everything clear?"

"Yes," I replied, meek and curious.

She was absolutely in earnest.

With this, Thüsis assumed a hurried, sinister voice, emphasizing her foreign accent, as she went on: "I found your cocaine. I know you want it. Come on, have a snort; I'll prepare it for you. Are you still reading Evola? If I were you, I'd take an interest in Marx; I'm afraid Fascism is on the way out. But who gives a damn. Here, it's ready. Have a line. How is it?"

"Good. It has a kind of kick."

"Give me a kiss. It's so irritating, the way I sometimes desire the substance of your tongue, soft and without any thickness. I can't figure out how a man of your age, blond, hairless, effeminate, surely homosexual, with blue eyes, can attract me. I have never allowed myself even to be touched by a man who wasn't Mediterranean, dark, sturdy, and hairy. I like overpowering men, a bit crude, men who like making love. I'm aroused by those strong, eager hands that know how to possess you: truck drivers, farmers . . . but you are passive, indifferent; if you don't sniff or don't drink, you can't get it up; and anyway I don't appeal to you . . ."

Thüsis had taken off the fur coat, the heat in the room was sultry, and she was sweating.

"Why are you in a sweat?"

"Because I was dancing, and anyway it isn't just sweat: it's oil. What if we took off that tiresome Wagner and danced a rumba or two?"

"And what if I didn't want to move, and seeing you all sweaty and greasy, I wanted to be with you in a little hotel in a tropical city, lying side by side, neither of us moving so as not to die of the heat? What if I asked you, to spare myself too much waste of energy, to masturbate me very slowly, while I do the same to you? And if I asked you to go into the kitchen and pretend that there is someone there, the manageress of this little hotel, say, and you ask her for a fan because your lover is dying of the heat? Then the manageress might tell you that there's only one fan and she had to give it to an elderly lady who's suffering from asthma, and then either with money or with physical provocation, you try to bribe her, for my sake, to give you the

51

fan. And finally you might succeed in arranging for the fan to be shared, half an hour for the lady with asthma and half an hour for us. Okay, Thüsis?"

"I don't understand this variation, but that doesn't matter; I'd just like to ask you, because I forgot to before, to call me Fleur. I'm a woman of thirty-five. I know you don't want to dance because you're a moralist, a bourgeois, and listening to Wagner seems to you more suitable to the insecurity of the moment. But that's wrong: you must enjoy yourself. Life is nothing, there's no future; now you enjoy yourself hugely, and while the other cowards do everything to try to prolong their lives, you think only of the desire of the moment. The bombs that fall become fireworks and the death-hypothesis means nothing to you. I am Fleur, a Nazi-Fascist, and I'm the official fiancée of a Fascist bigwig; you're a Jew and you know very well that I could report you, but you also know that I'm in love with you and my being in love flatters you and surprises you and the danger it involves at times is also an attraction. This is the first time you've fallen in love, only you never thought love was like this."

"The only thing that arouses me is your flesh, Fleur. Undress, put on more lipstick. Your beauty is underlined by the languid, greasy indolence that the heat causes. Then you become coarse-mouthed and desirable. Wagner doesn't suit me, either, in these circumstances, but I don't want a rumba; I'd rather we let the same tango go on playing, like our first night at the Pensione Europa. A tango helps, in bed. Maybe we should have a black-and-white TV and leave it on, along with the gramophone and the fan; we could also get some of those porn magazines you had in your room . . ."

"Claudio, I want you to leave your dressing gown half open, and with a glass of champagne in one hand, come to dance with me; even if death means nothing to us, the cold is awful, and in spite of the black market and the drugs, all these war years have weakened us, and so if we danced, the movement would provide us with a bit of warmth . . ."

"A dancer, mistress of a journalist of dubious talent, both motionless, passive, as time flows by monotonously . . ."

"Claudio, you aren't following me; you're doing it deliberately to humiliate me. I don't count at all, I don't exist; if I suggest a game to you, out of spite you have to play another, to make me feel that you have your independence, that our tastes aren't the same. You have to be aggressive, put me to the test . . ."

"Why, what are you talking about? It's no trick: it's masturbation."

"You see? What you're really saying is that, since we have different fantasies, we aren't made to be together. You know very well that I prefer the tango, but I wanted to see how you would react in a certain context, only you refused to pay any attention to me. Why wouldn't you accept my metamorphosis?"

"To be forty-year-olds takes substance, consistency, and you don't have it. Now, since it's not a question of acting, but arousing, it's not the same thing: your breasts are too firm, your lips too hard: it's a simple matter of flesh."

"I'm beginning to think you really are a pig; now listen to me carefully and you'll understand what I meant. You see this notebook bound in black crocodile?"

"Yes."

"Read the initials printed on it."

"T.T. Why?"

"T.T. stands for Tullio Treves. While I was shut up in my bedroom in your villa I got bored and accidentally I opened a desk drawer without thinking; I found this note-book, which is his diary. I took the liberty of reading it all, even though it's hard to decipher, because it aroused my curiosity and I couldn't stop. I still have to read some letters that were stuck in the diary."

"I don't see what my uncle Tullio's diary has to do with this melodramatic scenario that includes bombing and a fur coat in the middle of summer!"

When I woke up Thüsis had already gone out, and on the night table there was the crocodile notebook with a message: "Read it carefully, I'll be expecting you at the Pensione Europa. Thüsis."

I started reading immediately and I will copy out the passages that seemed to me most interesting.

PART THREE

The Diary

10

Turin, 25 December 1922

Christmas Day. The city is covered by a light blanket of snow, and looking out the window, I relive the glorious, sublime days of the taking of the capital. I would like to be again in that age-old, sunbaked city to help the companions in the building of that marvelous edifice that will heal our country and raise it to the rank of a great nation, with a glorious destiny. Instead, I am in my beloved Turin, in the house of my beloved parents, to spend the holidays with them.

Also in Turin are my brother Eugenio, my sister Elena, and her husband Löwenthal. The presence of this French socialist in the house irks me. After the thrilling, sleepless nights spent talking with my companions, after the enthusiasm of the glorious, historic days, it disturbs me to feel like an outsider in the house of my own parents. Out of politeness toward Löwenthal and also because of a certain snobbishness, at home only French is spoken, as if he could hardly be expected to condescend to understanding Italian. The Löwenthals are treated as special guests. All sorts of pains are taken to organize dinner parties for them, trips to museums, to the theater . . .

I'm also irritated because Löwenthal is so polite with me. He claims to be a socialist, but basically he's a man of the world, a man who loves power and the world of the powerful. And he looks down on us as poor provincials, benighted. Still, Elena has remained as dear as ever, and neither the Parisian life nor her husband's airs have changed her in any way.

Eugenio, on the contrary, is frivolous and thinks only of money and women; there's simply no talking with him. He seems to take no interest in anything, and whenever I try to steer him toward serious conversation, he makes some joke and changes the subject.

My relationship with Papa is ambiguous. I can feel that he's proud of my Roman exploits, but under the circumstances he has to assume a grave, almost reproachful demeanor, which he displays in silence. My mother has hinted that Eugenio and I should share an apartment, that we're too old to be still living at home. My assumption is that they would like to make me come back and live in Turin. My mother also said, in another conversation, that a young man like me, after such a glorious war and after my recent share in historic events, should make up his mind and marry and, with a healthy and productive life, consolidate the marvelous ideals of my young manhood.

Turin, June 1923

I take up this diary again, neglected over several months, which have been a turning point in my life. After the Christmas and New Year's holidays, I went back to Rome to see whether I should devote myself seriously to the country's political life and hence move to the Eternal City for good. I realized almost at once that the bellicose, youthful enthusiasm we *squadristi* demonstrated is not popular in today's Rome, where Mussolini wants to consolidate his political power and is seeking alliances and compromises with some members of the old political class; and only a few companions of the early days, his close collaborators from the beginning, certain men who helped finance and support the march on Rome, are involved in the government. For the moment I realize that my place is in Turin, where I can work much more usefully for the cause and the party.

The family regards with some suspicion the way I am dedicating myself to politics with such passion, and they insist that I should start working in the family business and should go regularly to the office with Papa, Uncle Massimo, and Eugenio. It's been decided that I will be in charge of certain real estate holdings and this will be extremely formative for my future. As I foresaw, they are also plotting a sensible marriage for me, and I believe they have chosen a girl from a good family: Allegra Montalcini. The Montalcinis have an excellent reputation in Turin Jewish society, but I've always felt uneasy around them, because they are too theoretical, all of them, and overrefined. I believe they're anti-Fascists, especially because they are always full of doubts, negative, and they look on whatever is new with distrust. They loathe anything vague, disorderly, and in Mussolini they still see the figure of an adventurer; they are unable to recognize his exceptional qualities. They can't realize that this man is inevitably fated to lead along the paths of glory the destiny of our beloved fatherland.

But since I'm a man of honor, an officer, and a dutiful son, I believe I'll be forced to accept certain responsibilities and certain obligations, even if they are in contrast with my true personality. The thing that torments me most is the thought of having to abandon a virile, solitary, and adventurous aspect of existence, to construct a more intimate and formal universe, based on criteria of upper middle class stability, which are remote from my present way of thinking. Luckily I still have some time to reflect ahead of me. I'll start working with Papa and Eugenio for a couple of months, and then in August I'll move to the mountains, alone, to ponder what avenue to take. Of one thing I'm sure: nothing will be able to alter my political ideals and my irrevocable decision to be first and foremost a Fascist, always ready to undertake any mission that might be assigned me in the interest of the nation and the party.

Valle d'Aosta, August 1927

Today I'm on holiday, in the Alpi Valdostane, with three young children. Allegra and I have been happily married for four years. The sublime part of my life with Allegra is that at the beginning we were both uneasy and discontent at having been virtually forced into marrying; but luckily we soon found that we were friends, kindred spirits, and love was born day by day, as time passed and the children came into the world. Shortly before marrying, I entered the family business, and now I can say that I have a certain knowledge of the real estate field. Naturally I haven't given up my ideals, which with tenacious and affectionate persuasion, I have made also the ideals of Allegra. It is a great satisfaction to witness the birth and the growth of a numerous Italian family, in this exceptional era, when gradually, in our peninsula, the splendors of an ancient civilization are being reborn, under the guidance, at once generous and ironclad, of Mussolini. In all these years, I've continued dedicating myself fervently to local political activity, taking part in various enterprises, sitting on committees, making regular trips to the capital. As a former officer, I've also had the privilege of two private audiences with His Royal Highness the Prince of Piedmont, a fine figure of an officer and intellectual.

On three different occasions I've also had the extraordinary good fortune to meet Mussolini personally, twice at party rallies and once at a meeting. Naturally I have close friends in the Turin party leadership. Both my father, before his premature death, and my brother Eugenio, who followed him as head of the family, have always had great respect for my double activity as businessman and militant Fascist.

As could have been predicted, once the first distrust of the new and revolutionary aspect of the regime was past, the vast majority of the Italians, you can say, have lined up on Mussolini's side.

During these years I have also had a fundamental experience in the life of a man: I have become a father three times, and this fills me with hope.

My parents sensed the genuine material that existed in me and they led me intelligently toward a proper order that has allowed me to fulfill myself. I must say that at the beginning I had some reservations about Allegra, because I was afraid she would try to inculcate in me the principles of the Montalcini household. I was mistaken. Allegra has proved a fine wife and has taken naturally to her new role as Baroness Treves. I don't want to sound boastful, but I would say sincerely that we are a very popular and sought-after couple in Turin society.

Valle d'Aosta, August 1927

Exaltation of nature, enchanting landscapes. Excursion into the forest with a group of party companions who have come to pay me a visit. Dancing in the evening, and great high spirits. I am rereading the prose works of our Bard. Stupendous pages! In literature Italy is reburgeoning and producing beautiful works both in prose and in poetry.

In the country, September 1927

I have resumed working and I commute every day between Turin and the country. It thrills me to return toward the fields at evening. At night I listen to music. This winter I am seriously going to go back to the piano. I hope my children have a good ear for music.

Turin, June 1928

I've had the very great honor of being received, in Rome, by His Excellency Bottai. I knew he had been a fine soldier and that he is a statesman of exceptional quality, but I would never have thought he was so refined, cultivated, and rich in creative ideas. He told me that he felt a kinship with me because I shared his opinion that, to perfect the functioning of the country, it is indispensable to encourage and develop cultural activities.

I don't want to seem vain, but the Honorable Bottai also congratulated me on those few little articles of musical criticism that, in the time stolen from the numerous obligations of my life, I have managed to send occasionally to the *Gazzetta del Popolo*.

He urged me to continue and asked me if, every now and then, I would be willing to contribute to his magazine,

Critica Fascista. I still can't get over this honor. I've been back in Turin a few days, and I still am filled with the euphoria I brought with me from the capital.

Paris, March 1931

For several days I have been staying in my brother-in-law Löwenthal's house in Paris. I've had a trivial accident, and my sister Elena, very affectionately, is taking care of me. I came to Paris to try to help my fellow Fascists living in France to find some ways of lessening the disturbance created by some little groups of political exiles and Italian anti-Fascist intellectuals living here in Paris, or in London or New York. We worked out an excellent plan of co-ordination and future strategy, and I still had a half-day to go to the Louvre and see the Delacroixs and the Géricaults. On the eve of my departure, I stupidly wounded myself while opening a bottle of iced champagne; it blew up in my hands. So I was advised to rest a few days. Elena's husband is a great friend of Léon Blum, and as the years pass he is becoming more and more that great enlightened bourgeois that he has always wanted to be, since his youth.

Turin, June 1931

I am in town, working hard, and honored that *Critica Fascista* has printed a brief article of mine. With a hand-written letter the Honorable Bottai sent me his congrat-ulations.

As usual we will spend the summer first in the country, then in Valle d'Aosta. We have another son, just born, and I believe it's best to be cautious.

There is talk that Eugenio wants to marry a German

ballerina. He met her during a trip to Germany, and seems to be in love with her. Knowing him, I have a hard time believing this.

1 January 1935

It's strange, the way I've neglected writing in this notebook for a long time. Whenever I come upon it, I always feel some emotion. Even though I've published, during the past few years, a little volume of verse, a history of the Risorgimento, a little book on mysticism, as well as my memoirs of Caporetto and Vittorio Veneto, this notebook has a special value for me, the expression in writing of events and emotions, without any other purpose. How many things have happened in these years! The splendid fulfillment, year by year, of our regime. The tangible results can be seen in the schools, in the creation of monumental works, the reclamation of whole regions of the peninsula; even in the health of the Italian people, who can finally feel proud, under the Duce's guidance. I am very busy with Turin Fascism and I confess that I am sorry to hear that the regime, in imitation of Germany, is beginning to become racist and anti-Semitic. I don't want to attach too much importance to trivial reports printed in papers like the *Tevere,* and I won't deign to consider the racism of fanatics like Interlandi. These are sporadic cases, far more frequent in other countries, like France and Germany. Mussolini has never been a racist; he has only, rightly, criticized the defeatist or rebellious attitude of some of my coreligionists. I am fully aware that in Turin, in a certain intellectual ambience, negative, defeatist notions are current, openly anti-Fascist; and among those intellectuals, unfortunately, there are some Jews. These Jewish intellectuals are dangerous fomenters of the Zionist notion, the idea of giving the Jews a promised land; as if it were possible to transplant Germans, French, Poles, Russians, and Italians to a British protectorate inhabited by Arabs, and make it into a Jewish state. It would be much simpler if these hotheads could be silenced, with the punishment they deserve, and the valorous people of Israel were to be assimilated, as is the case in Italy, for example, and were to strive to be above all citizens of the nation in which they live and work. I am happy to see, here in Turin, the new enterprise of a group of Jewish Fascist intellectuals, who publish a magazine, *Nostra Bandiera,* which in a sense supports my opinions on Zionism and indicates the proper attitude for Jews in the world.

But since the magazine is virtually an official organ of the Jewish community, it is obviously more moderate on the question of assimilation. Still, it fights Zionism courageously. It would be too bad if, because of a few subversives, the overwhelming majority of Italian and Fascist Jews were to undergo an unjust fate.

Hitler's Germany, on the contrary, is openly anti-Semitic. It's pathetic to see these families of German Jews who have come as refugees to our country, famous for its hospitality. They are received and integrated as quickly as possible in our working world.

It is New Year's morning, and everything is silent around me. More and more, I understand why I am so fond of this notebook, where I express things that public position would prevent me from saying otherwise.

Florence, April 1937

I have brought my two older children to Florence; I want them to visit properly this city filled with incomparable gems. I believe it's important for them to see works of art of inestimable value in this sober, austere city. At times I am moved, when I think of the handful of us in Rome in 1922 and how today Italy is an empire respected throughout the world.

I have just returned from the war in Ethiopia, where I signed up as a volunteer officer. Being at headquarters, at the side of Marshal Badoglio, whom I had the honor to meet when I was with General Scipioni at Vittorio Veneto, was an immense emotion. On this occasion I had to disapprove of the contemptible attitude of Eugenio, who refused to take part in this action as an Italian Fascist volunteer, using his work as a pretext. Eugenio has too many dealings with the United States and England; and he says that if the offenses against the Jews were ever to increase, he would leave Italy. Eugenio has become a defeatist, since marrying that German dancer, and he thinks of nothing but accumulating money. He is overconcerned by the rumors of anti-Semitism in circulation, and being a great egoist, he is thinking of where he could emigrate and continue his business undisturbed. He says that the idea of the empire has gone to the Duce's head, and he has too grandiose plans, and furthermore too close a friendship with Hitler could have dramatic consequences for Italy.

He doesn't understand that it is right for the Fascist dictatorship or others inspired by Fascism to be friends and allies. He refuses to understand that the Duce possesses the true warrior spirit and that in him there is also a strong sense of independence and freedom of action.

I am sure that the destinies of Italy and of Germany will remain separate. At this moment we are offering a magnificent example of solidarity, as our volunteer legions fight at the side of brave Spanish soldiers to restore order and create a strong government in a country that is shattered and adrift.

During these past few years I have returned to Paris several times, but my relations with Löwenthal are spoiled. He is still close to Blum; he says that Italy is a warmongering country, dangerously anti-Semitic, and that Mussolini is leading us toward catastrophe.

Elena is saddened that there is no longer the old association between me and her husband, but still she comes to visit me at my hotel with Miriam, an intelligent and very likable girl.

In Turin I often play four hands with Allegra, and I would say that music and the mountains in the summer are the sweetest pleasures of this strong and busy life.

It's extraordinary to live in a country where, gradually, individualism is disappearing and where the life of all citizens is directed toward the common construction of something. In Italy we are finally breathing an air of strength and respect. The country's agriculture is flourishing, we are fighting for the citizens' health, for education and culture. I think with pride of Italo Balbo's air fleet and those young and bold airmen who have won such glory for Italy.

7 January 1939

The racial laws have become a reality. It seems that even His Excellency Bottai, in the session of the Grand Council, was a firm supporter. They have been promulgated in order to strengthen our relations with the Germans on the Jewish question, but especially — because of the numerous races that now make up our empire — to prevent mixing of blood and to protect Italian purity.

By a quirk of fate, this law also strikes me and my family; and I have had to reflect at length about it. My brother Eugenio, opportunist and traitor as I knew he was, emigrated to the United States last October, though I had done everything possible to dissuade him. Now I, Tullio Treves, baron, silver medal for wartime valor, officer at the front and with the high command, participant in the march on Rome, Fascist militant from the start of the movement, respected and honored by the party, also belong to the same religion as any other Jew, and my children will have to leave the Liceo d'Azeglio and transfer to the Hebrew school. I cannot carry on any professional activities or occupy positions in the party, and at forty-two, I find myself with nothing to do. I could take advantage of my early membership in the Fascist party to avoid undergoing the same treatment as ordinary Jews or the Zionists and Bolshevik Jews, but it seems indecorous to me. I know that many are doing it, but it seems to me a somehow dishonorable escape. So I am an Italian deprived of his civil rights and even of his condition as an Italian. This doesn't distress me: my individual fate means nothing to me. The only thing I have never understood is why it was my fate to be a born a member of a minority for which I feel no particular fondness or affinity.

Though I have chosen to submit to the "laws" like the others and not try to hide my background in any way, politically I share the attitude of the Honorable Bottai, who is not personally a racist, but places the country's interest and the government's above everything else, showing that he is a true statesman. There is no doubt that if there were to be a conflict against the other European nations, it would be Italy's interest to join German military might, which will defeat all the other countries, puffed up with hot air and unprepared for a real war. In this eventuality, it will be deeply humiliating for me, to be unable to go and fight.

The necessity of making some sacrifices in our daily life, such as reducing our *train de vie,* only makes me feel young again.

In this period I reject the thought of solidarity with the other Jews, simply because a momentary historical situation links us. In any event, I remain a loyal Fascist.

For that matter, I am sure that after a brief conflict, which will surely be victorious for Italy, things will change, and certain temporary laws and measures will disappear. I hate pietism and can't bear for non-Jewish friends to express sympathy. I will devote this period of my life to deeper meditation and I will find consolation in music. I know that these few lines, in the face of such a serious problem, may seem poor and superficial, but I feel that I will have the time to delve more profoundly into certain thoughts of mine.

23 January 1939

On the train for Paris, going to see Elena. I have heard that she and her husband are thinking of taking refuge in Switzerland, with their daughter, and I would like to know why, aware as I am of Löwenthal's deep attachment to France.

Eugenio's decision to leave Italy was quite another matter. He couldn't remain idle; he is a born businessman, and therefore he has moved to a New York bank. My decision to remain is irrevocable. We will only have to adjust temporarily our way of life, but this can only make us more united. I prefer this to having to undergo exile.

These racial laws to me seem supremely demagogical, and the Italian people are either indignant or indifferent. The children are getting along well at the Hebrew school, where a number of distinguished university professors, having been dismissed from their chairs, have come to teach.

Paris, 3 February 1939

Elena never tires of insisting that the situation is grave and that I and Allegra and the children should emigrate with them. The plan would be first to move to Zurich and then, perhaps, to the United States. Löwenthal has been very frank, straightforward. He told me that as a father it is my duty, whatever my political opinions may be, to think first of the safety of my wife and children. He painted a dramatic picture of a Europe under Nazi domination in which there would be no hope of salvation for a Jew. He said that Mussolini is surely a more intelligent and moderate man than Hitler, but German power will in the end make Italy a secondary nation and to survive, the Italians would have to agree to all sorts of compromises, including more strict and thorough application of the racial laws. I thanked Löwenthal very much for his intelligent and affectionate attempts to protect me. I told him that I realized how painful it must be for him to leave France, but as for me, I will stay in Italy. My determination to remain in Italy made Elena burst into desperate sobs. She gripped my shoulders, seized my arms, and tried to convince me. "At least Allegra and the children!" she kept saying, or "If you want to commit suicide, go ahead; but you have no right to drag your children down with you." I replied, also speaking for the children, that we would never emigrate unless things became unbearable, and then, at that point, if there was really nothing to be done, we would always find somebody willing to rescue us.

We parted sadly, with emotion. Sadly, because in Elena's eyes I read the fear that the war might separate us forever.

June 1939

This year we are leaving for a three months' vacation in Valle d'Aosta. It will be very good for my health and for the children's. I would like to release the inner torments of these last few years, abandoning myself to nature, to its harsh and wild aspect. I should listen more to noises, be more sensitive to smells, walk and contemplate the mountains.

Prato San Desiderio, 3 July 1939

I've been in the Alps for a month and I feel regenerated. I try to find once more the physical shape of a Fascist man. These last years I have let myself go. I became fat, and I felt my face and stomach bloat. Here I eat little, walk a great deal, and play tennis.

Prato San Desiderio, 27 July 1939

I've spent a delightful week. On an excursion Allegra and I met a splendid couple, with whom we have made friends.

He is a well-known Fascist official, of the younger generation, and at the moment he occupies a position of great responsibility in Bologna. I believe he comes from Romagna, at least to judge by his accent. He has a very virile bearing; he is tall, with dark hair and dark skin. She, who is apparently his mistress, speaks Italian with a foreign accent. She is blond, with almost perfect features, and wonderful blue eyes, big and smiling.

They are both athletic; they know and love the mountains. He rides and also plays excellent tennis. He is one of the Fascists (and I believe there are many like him) who regard the racial laws with detachment and treat Jews normally, not even referring to the situation. I asked His Excellency if he thinks Italy will go into the war against the "Pluto-Judaic-Masonic" powers. He smiled, rightly avoiding an answer he's in no position to give. Italy's war destiny seems to lie exclusively in the hands of the Duce, whose farseeing eyes will inspire the decision most opportune for the nation.

7 August 1939

The Bolognese official's woman is named Céleste; she says she's French and was educated in Paris, London, and Florence. She stayed on another week by herself, and we saw her often. I must confess that I am not indifferent to her fascination, and I somewhat envy that official: free to live with a woman so beautiful and interesting.

Interesting is the wrong word: Céleste is an unpredictable woman. She can be elusive, flattering, polite, rude. She praises then condemns, then is silent, then very witty. I certainly can't say that she lacks personality. Furthermore, she's a true Fascist, in the way that Fascism was at its dawn: strong, aggressive, frank. She pays no heed to what people will say. For the moment, besides our political ideals, we share a passion for the mountains.

11 August 1939

Yesterday evening Céleste left. We exchanged addresses and she said she won't fail to come and see us in Turin.

15 August 1939

The mid-August holiday is always sad, and I feel gloomy. I miss Céleste. I believe I've developed a crush on her, and now that she's gone, the mountains, which seemed so glorious and splendid to me, look merely like insignificant rocks. This mood may stem also from the approach of our departure and the fact that after the tenth of August the days grow shorter and you already sense that autumn is coming closer.

Turin, 23 November 1939

Italy is still neutral. I see in the paper that in January the Bolognese official we met in the mountains will be transferred to Turin, on a special assignment. I wonder if Céleste will remember us?

18 March 1940

Céleste telephoned. She says she would like to come and see us one evening, incognito.

1 April 1940

Last night Céleste and the official came to supper in corso Fiume. We chatted pleasantly about everything, except the war. While we were seated at table, I felt Céleste's shoe against mine; I moved my foot, but a moment later I felt hers again. I left mine where it was; or rather I moved it a little closer, and she did the same. The sweet sensation that between us something has begun. Perhaps I have a beautiful mistress.

This morning I looked at myself carefully in the mirror,

and even though my face is relaxed, I've lost some weight and toned myself up, I'm still far from being Adonis. And yet in those furtive contacts there was amorous desire: I'm sure of it. Nobody noticed anything, and I can't really believe I am loved or desired by such a woman.

19 April 1940

Met Céleste at Baratti's. We ordered aperitifs and slowly stroked hands, looking into each other's eyes.

"Tullio, je suis folle de vous et je veux vous retrouver au lit; je veux que vous me serriez dans vos bras. Depuis que je vous connais il y a quelque chose de louche et de mystérieux qui m'attire chez vous."

"I'll find a place for our love, under an assumed name."

"Tu m'aimes?"

"Do you realize the danger you're risking? Un juif?"

"J'aime le danger et les juifs sont des amants merveilleux."

11 May 1940

There is much talk of war, but I pay no attention to it. I live in my family circle, but I think only of my furtive meetings with Céleste in various cafés in the city.

I have found an apartment free at the beginning of June in corso Vittorio. Unfortunately there is a movie theater in the same building; I can't say it's a very pleasant place.

9 June 1940

We have inaugurated the apartment in corso Vittorio, making love, still dressed, in the big Empire bed in our new bedroom. To be sure, as Céleste says, these racial laws that forbid me to work are a great stroke of luck for a pair of passionate lovers.

The apartment is almost empty, a bit dark, and we can hear the sound of the movies. I love this blond woman who makes me forget everything. Yesterday she told me she would bring me some cocaine. I've never taken any; I've just read about it in novels, and I'm curious.

11 June 1940

The Duce has declared war on France and England; our troops are preparing to conquer the territory including Nice that was once Italian, and they are fighting effectively at the side of our German ally. This is more or less the tenor of the official communiqué. I feel thrust aside, and I don't believe our troops are behaving in the way I would have expected.

Still, I felt a great emotion on hearing "Conquer! We shall conquer!" said by the Duce in a magnificent speech addressed to all Italians from the balcony of piazza Venezia.

After that speech, almost like a robot, I walked along via Po, deserted and dimly lighted, but at a certain point, from a side street, a large group of Blackshirts appeared, proceeding almost at a run, singing "Giovinezza" and other Fascist anthems. At first I felt old, dreary, outcast, but then, on a mad impulse, I followed them, too, at the same pace, under the arcades, and like them I sang "Giovinezza." Nobody could recognize me, or at worst they would have taken me for a drunk. After years, to sing those songs that were once my *daily bread* filled me with a great, youthful euphoria, which later in the evening turned into melancholy.

16 July 1940

On vacation in the mountains. This year Céleste has gone to the Lido in Venice, so won't be coming here. As if that weren't enough to make me gloomy, I've received a letter from Eugenio in the United States: pages and pages of warnings and insults, ultimatums, and lots of "immediately or it will be too late." He calls me a criminal because, in my insane faith in Fascism, I am sentencing my loved ones to certain death. He threatens me, saying I should do everything possible to send the children to Switzerland. What a strange way of thinking Eugenio has! Italy, with Germany, is now master of half of Europe, and that defeatist threatens me and accuses me of being a criminal father.

25 August 1940

I can't take any more of this useless life, of playing games in society, athletic activity, and long walks. All groups, families, large or small, put my patience to a severe test. I can't wait to go back to Turin.

November 1940

Céleste has told me that she will have to visit me less often because her lover is becoming suspicious, not of me in particular, but because she seems to be eluding him. Allegra knows nothing of my double life. The war continues victoriously, but the death of Balbo was a real tragedy and has left a void that can't be filled. The rumor is that the Duce had him killed: I don't consider this possible. In Turin daily life seems normal except that there are a number of refugees and food is hard to find.

December 1940

I am lying on the bed in corso Vittorio. Céleste has just gone, and outside it's snowing. Our relationship is intense; we thirst for each other. Besides making love, we adore talking, telling stories of our past, daydreaming. We look toward our future with terror, and we listen to a great deal of Wagner. Céleste has repressed sexual instincts that she releases only with me. I asked her how she could be attracted to a pink little man with a slightly porcine face. She says that is precisely what attracts her. She's confessed, too, that another quality of mine that drives her crazy is my irresponsibility. The fact that I haven't run away, that I don't worry, don't take any steps to protect myself: all this fascinates her.

She is amused by the contrast between my respectable appearance and my spirit, which, on the contrary, is basically corrupted by decadent tastes and my morbid passion for art. Céleste insists that my blind loyalty to Fascism is a way of disguising certain homosexual tendencies and my fear of falling otherwise into a dangerous individualism, in a period of history when only the masses are accepted and we assume mass tastes. She says I'm eccentric and presumptuous. She declares that if Fascism hadn't been the only alternative — and the most obvious — I would probably have become an anti-Fascist, but my perversion drove me to adopt, in an absurdly yielding way, the horrible aesthetic taste of the regime.

I let her say and do what she likes; she doesn't outrage my ideals in any way. Though I continue to remain faithful to my cause, something flaccid and venomous has taken possession of me.

January 1942

Grim news all along the line.

My oldest boy died of typhus, a tragedy that has turned Allegra completely mute. She has shut herself away in the country, in a deaf, suicidal grief. It is horrible to lose a child, and I suffer for the torment of Allegra, who now wants to send the other children to Switzerland at all costs. The Löwenthals, who have settled in Zurich, could look after them and assume responsibility.

Löwenthal wasn't all that mistaken, it turns out, about the future fate of our country. I am putting up no opposition to the idea that the children, if they like, and also possibly Allegra, should go and stay for a while in Switzerland.

At this dire moment, full of sorrow and indecision, I miss more than ever the presence of Céleste. Ever since she left for Rome, I have felt ill at times, with the need of her body, of our trivial conversations, our private language made up of French, Italian, and German, spoken with the most absurd accents. I miss Céleste's way of always looking at everything as if it were a practical joke.

February 1942

Allegra has become my enemy. She lives in the country, swears she will never set foot again in the city, and is preparing to move to the mountains, near the border. She says that the war is lost; the Germans have dragged our Alpine troops and our cavalry into a desperate fight against the Russians, not to mention the war against the United States.

"It's obvious. If you just read *War and Peace*," Allegra

declares, "and you learn that the Russians are merciless and invincible. Eternal Russia can't be conquered."

Allegra wants to send the children to safety at any price. I don't know how to react, and I am living through empty days, in the little house in corso Fiume where I listen to Wagner and in corso Vittorio, where I lie inert on the bed, hoping that Céleste will appear. I love her desperately, and I seem to care nothing at all about the fate of the world. Allegra can do what she thinks best with the children.

August 1942

For the first time in my life I am spending the whole month of August in Turin. Céleste and I are alone. Allegra has gone to live in the mountains, in the constant hope of crossing the border any day. Céleste and I spend almost all the time in the house. The heat and boredom weigh on us and Céleste is constantly blaming me for keeping her in this revolting place and not taking her on a holiday. At night there is the curfew and we enjoy it when the alarm sounds and we don't go down to the shelter but wait for death in bed. Allegra says I'm mad not to join her.

26 November 1942

Terrible times. Carpet bombings, and every day Turin seems more destroyed. Will we survive? There are moments of genuine terror!

Christmas 1942

Allegra is still in the mountains; two of the children have crossed into Switzerland; Céleste is in Taranto, and we are united by a frequent correspondence, in which I sign myself Cavalier Luigi Podda and she, Contessa Ada Louise Vidal. For the rest, I keep alive in Turin, dream, listen to Wagner, read Evola and old speeches of the Duce. When parades are announced in the paper, I join the crowd because I feel a kind of joy, singing the old anthems in the street. I go from moments of depression to moments of euphoria.

April 1943

Received a letter from Céleste: "I miss you day and night. I spend hours of boredom and irritation at the side of my handsome and weak hero who senses that at this point the tide of the war is turning. He cries because he says I love only the powerful and therefore I will soon leave him for a victorious American officer. But instead I think of you, my little circumcised man, who, if you weren't such a fool and didn't declare yourself a Fascist, in a few years' time would be a hero-victim, member of a wickedly persecuted minority. I'm about to come back to Turin; wait for me in corso Vittorio. The hero has been transferred again, on a special war mission. I love you. Ada Louise."

August 1943

Have been to see Allegra and my daughter in the mountains.

They barely speak to me and look at me with contempt. Allegra has found out about Céleste and blames this vulgar affair of mine for the ruin of our family.

The Americans have landed in Sicily. After a historic meeting of the Grand Council, the Fascist regime has fallen.

Mussolini is in prison, and Italy is in the hands of His Majesty and Marshal Badoglio. I really don't know what to think.

October 1943

The Italian Social Republic has been established, under Mussolini; but actually we are occupied by the Germans. The Jews are being tracked down, and Céleste is again in Turin. The city is devastated by the Allied bombings, and the two of us, irresponsible, recklessly continue our erotic games. To amuse herself she threatens to report me to the Gestapo; I laugh and dare her to do it.

December 1943

I can't understand why Allegra keeps postponing her escape across the border. Perhaps in her heart of hearts she is sorry to abandon me. She has set up a family meeting, she says we all have to meet and decide. So she has asked our two boys to come back from Switzerland: a pointless and dangerous idea, it seems to me. In any case I'll go and see them for Christmas. Céleste swears that if I move an inch from Turin, she'll turn me in, report my whole family, and will have us all shot.

PART FOUR

An Investigation Begins

11

I must say that it was a long, hard job, penetrating those pages written in an almost illegible — and always changing — hand. What a strange, contorted person that Tullio Treves was! What interested me most was his women. The unexpected Céleste, that angelic and perverse creature, who may very well have turned him in, out of jealousy; and my aunt Allegra. Tullio was in love with her, too; in fact, in the end, he left Céleste and joined her. This Allegra Montalcini, who according to the family was a "fine woman," seems to have a hint of madness, a complicated character. When Aunt Allegra discovers the thing between Céleste and Uncle Tullio and realizes that her husband has drawn her and the children into a mad, dangerous situation, she leaves him, flees to the Swiss border, but until the end she waits for him and even makes her sons come back from Switzerland.

Plunged in these various, conflicting thoughts, I started walking along via Po, under the same arcades where Tullio secretly followed the Blackshirts singing "Giovinezza." On the night war was declared, there were no bright shop windows, idle kids, motorbikes. Though it was smaller then, I have the impression that Turin was a more austere and less provincial city than now.

Perhaps Thüsis has found something in the letters about that Céleste, which will help me discover if she was the one who reported my uncle and aunt and cousins. But if this were so, then Uncle Tullio would be doubly guilty for the death of his family. He was the one to provoke it, to pull the trigger!

As I was climbing the steps to the Pensione Europa I ran into Aunt Miriam. I didn't mention the diary to her, but I asked her if she knew my grandfather Dimitri. I told her I had written to ask him to come and see my mother before it was too late. She replied that I had done the right thing, she knew Grandfather Dimitri only by sight, but she knew how close he and my mother had always been. She would surely be happy to see him! Having said this, my aunt briskly excused herself and hurried off. Her way of moving, the aura of perfume and powder around her made me think of an ocean liner leaving the harbor, emitting great puffs of smoke and explosions.

I found Thüsis lying on her bed, looking exhausted, a cigarette in her mouth. On seeing me, she said immediately: "Well?"

"Fleur, Céleste: who was this woman? If she's still alive and she was the one who reported Uncle Tullio, she should be found, to avenge the memory of those innocent cousins. Have you read the letters?"

"Yes, give me a kiss; I'm horrified."

"What is it?"

"Apart from one letter, dated 1939, addressed to a lawyer in Turin named Morpurgo whom Tullio covers with insults because of his defeatist, Zionist ideas, the rest is an erotic correspondence, from spring of '43, in which Céleste calls herself Ada Louise Vidal, and Tullio signs himself Luigi Podda."

"I believe Tullio mentions these letters in the diary: when she's in Taranto."

"Yes, but reading them, I may have discovered something incredible."

"Namely?"

"For the most part the letters are full of little tricks and lies, meant to make each other jealous. For example, Ada Louise talks about a nephew of hers, by the name of Foulk. She describes this very handsome man, slender and athletic, and uses his physical qualities to tease 'Podda Treves.' I'll read you part of one letter: 'I've learned that my nephew is fighting on the side of the enemy, in North Africa. Do you think we must suffer a hero's fate, the pair of us slaughtered because it's not right to change your mind? Can it be said that this beautiful young man who is fighting for the victory of the Western democracies is an enemy of ours?'

"Cavalier Podda answers her, irritated, that it doesn't seem right in his view to cite a specific instance, such as that of her nephew, to define what an enemy is or isn't. As far as he is concerned, Luigi Podda repeats that he will never deny his allegiance, he will always be a fierce opponent of the democratic idea, and he will never alter his ideas to suit the times. Besides the constant descriptions of her 'beautiful' nephew, Ada Louise mentions, with words like *slave, handmaiden, attendant,* a woman: Esther Moscati, probably Tullio's domestic, and accuses him, saying, for example: 'She obeys you like a devoted slave, demeaning herself to satisfy your every whim and every vice.'

"I have deduced that Esther Moscati was probably a Jewish girl, who because of the racial laws came and did the cleaning in the corso Vittorio apartment. Céleste is constantly suspecting her of being 'Tullio's mistress.' "

"So there are three possible sources of information: Foulk, Morpurgo, and this Moscati! Naturally if Céleste is still alive, it would be indispensable to meet her."

"Did you pay attention to what I said to you about the letters and the young Foulk business? Doesn't there seem something strange about it? What did you think of the diary?"

"I would never have thought a man could be like Tullio Treves. A life of passions, extremes, repressions. It's history that assails him. He deplores, but he doesn't rebel . . . only a bit of immorality, irresponsibility, when he and Céleste play games during the air raids. Otherwise, there's history, the mountains, or his wife, persecutions or typhus. But you can't help liking him! Yesterday evening, in piazza Carignano, you were so good putting on that angel face! Fleur was a lot like Céleste. Too bad we don't have a photograph!"

"You know my last name, don't you?"

"I don't remember. Why?"

"Foulk. Like Céleste's nephews, who could be Daffy and Bill. They fought in Africa, then in the Italian campaign. I've heard lots of family talk about an eccentric aunt who moved to Italy and became a militant Fascist when Mussolini came to power. I know she was always considered *maudite* and Daffy was the only one who remained friendly."

"It can't be! You don't mean to tell me that Céleste, that woman who may have had my uncle killed and his whole family, is your aunt! It's too much!"

"I'm not sure her name was Céleste, but I think it was. And there's her Fascism, the handsome officer, the name Foulk . . . I absolutely must ask Uncle Bill. Unfortunately,

I seem to remember he wasn't on good terms with her. He's too social and opportunistic to admit to having a relative that might cause him embarrassment."

"It seems impossible! Forty years ago, then, here in Turin there was this big love story between my uncle and your aunt! I hope it's not true. Not that I really believe she reported them, but the suspicion remains."

"I admit I feel a bit shaken, especially after the Fleur game."

"You should go and talk with your uncle and try to discover if the two witnesses mentioned in the letters, that lawyer Morpurgo and Esther Moscati, are still alive. I really wouldn't want to learn that an aunt of yours . . . But if she's still alive, and if she really did it, then I have somehow to avenge the memory of Aunt Allegra and my cousins. Don't you think?"

"It's a nasty story, but for the moment, as you say, the important thing is to find out if Céleste is my aunt, if she's still alive; and the witnesses should be questioned."

12

I went to meet my grandfather Dimitri at the station. He was as I had imagined, dressed in white linen, carrying a little, ancient suitcase of reddish leather, also wearing a broad-brimmed panama, and brown-and-white shoes. He came toward me along the platform, hardly pressing on his black cane with the lapis lazuli handle; and looking at me at once, he said: "My dear, what a tragedy!"

"Yes, it is."

"How can it be? Such a young woman!"

We left his case at the pension, and he insisted I take him to Mama immediately. In the car he asked me a number of questions about my life, and I spoke to him about Thüsis.

I took him into my mother's room and I watched them talk. Grandfather murmured and held her hand; she smiled, to let him know that she recognized him and was happy he had come. Grandfather came out of the room distraught, and on the drive back, he did nothing but repeat, "My dear, what a tragedy, poor woman."

That evening Thüsis and I had supper with Grandfather and Aunt Miriam.

At first we chatted about this and that. Miriam and

Grandfather tried to remember how they first met, then they began talking of my mother, and then Grandfather asked Thüsis what she was doing in Turin. Grandfather seemed to send her into ecstasy and she told him all about Tanya and the dance school. She talked to him without smoking and she looked at him with wide eyes.

His curiosity was aroused by Thüsis's inflamed way of speaking. I suffered because I was only one part of her life, one among other things: not everything, as I would have liked to be.

I felt that I loved the two of them and envied them their way of conversing, both beautiful and very pure, intense and intelligent. I realized that I was jealous of their independence. With me, she had never been open in this way; she had given me enthusiasm, erotism, strong sensations, but she had never looked at me with that spontaneous intensity.

Thüsis seemed to be no longer aware of me; at that moment she was thinking of herself, of the dance, of Grandfather: I didn't exist.

Aunt Miriam had also joined in the conversation, and the three of them talked until Thüsis asked Grandfather: "Did you ever know a woman named Céleste Foulk?"

"I certainly did!" Grandfather replied. "But you —? How did you know her?"

"I never knew her, but she's my great-aunt, and since I know she lived in Paris, I was wondering —"

"She was a beautiful woman; she looked like Greta Garbo. I was introduced to her in Nice: I remember her as if it were yesterday, sitting at the bar of the Negresco. And then I met her a few months later, in Paris, in the home of some Galician friends. She declared that she was the widow of a Fascism and an Italy that only she knew, and that would never exist again."

"What's Aunt Céleste like?"

"Now that you tell me she's your aunt, I can see a resemblance, perhaps even in personality. But each of us chooses his role, and if yours is the role of ballerina, hers was the role of the shady character, the perverse adventuress. She was acting, but she did it so naturally that her role became her real self."

Aunt Miriam spoke up, irritated at having been temporarily excluded: "Dimitri, don't you feel you're letting your taste for novels run away with you, speaking of this woman? You're a romantic, and you've idealized her as if she were the synthesis of all your dreams about women . . ."

"I can see that you take as fiction everything I want to believe is reality. The truth of the matter is that I wasn't expecting my grandson and his friend, in this Turin restaurant, to lead me to speak of Céleste."

It seemed to me, from his description of her, that my grandfather Dimitri had really known Céleste, but this wasn't the right moment to go any further into the matter.

A few days after that meal as I was strolling alone with my grandfather, I asked him if he had really known Céleste or if his story had been just the fruit of his imagination. I added that it was important for me to know, because Thüsis was trying to track down this lady.

With a look of surprise, Grandfather answered: "Do you think a man of my age can joke about something as serious as the last great love of his life? I allowed your aunt Miriam to be sarcastic because I'm a man of the world, and also because it's something very personal that is no business of hers. If Céleste really is Thüsis's aunt, I hope you do find some trace of her because I would be curious to know what became of her."

"The coincidences between your Céleste, the black widow of a Fascism forever vanished, and Thüsis's Céleste, mistress of two Fascists, the blond adventuress, shady and very elegant, make me think that it absolutely has to be the same person."

"I remember her very precisely, and I'm sure her name was Céleste Foulk. For that matter, she also talked to me about her family. Corsican, French, American. She always spoke adoringly about two very handsome and brave nephews, sons of her brother, who was a boring moralist with rigid principles. She would often describe Italy to me as a mythical, enchanting country, now lost forever, and she insisted she never wanted to go back. I don't know why, but I remember her favorite cities were Bologna and Turin.

"I sincerely hope Thüsis manages to find her! They really do resemble each other, you know. Besides their coloring and the shape of the face, it's incredible how there are moments when the expression seems the same. I wouldn't want to misjudge, but I seem to have noticed that Thüsis's moods change frequently: she can concentrate completely on a subject or can be totally vague, absent. Before you wheedle her out of a sudden bad humor, she is already in high spirits, and the sadness has vanished. Céleste was the same: she would be grouchy for a moment, then she would look at you with surprise and ask: 'What's wrong? Are you in a bad humor?' or else, 'Do I look ugly?' and I would say, 'Why, what are you talking about?' And she would say, 'I don't know: you look at me, but you aren't saying anything.'

"It seems to me you've found yourself a remarkable girl."

"But, Grandfather, don't you think this changeability can be wearing, dangerous."

"See here, Alberto Claudio, it depends on how you act. To love that kind of woman, you have to love women, realize they're made in a different way. All their emphasis on beauty, their moods have to be accepted serenely. You can't understand why a beautiful woman can ask you, 'Am I ugly?' But she does it because there are moments when it annoys her to feel less beautiful, or because she wants to hear someone say, 'No, you look stupendous! You're the most beautiful of all!' The moodiness of the women we love is a stimulus to us to cheer them up. Woman is man's only real stimulus, his motor. That's why all the great poets had a muse."

Grandfather spoke in a low voice, with affection. He reassured me, calmed my apprehensions about Thüsis.

"But how can we know if a woman really loves us?"

"By loving her with our whole self."

"And if we lose her?"

"I don't want to seem old and pedantic, but it's like dogma, like a true faith. A man must experience his love without reservations, with trust, doing everything he can to make sure the woman's love comes to him, then . . . Life has too many mysteries, and it would be futile to try to understand them. Lying for a good end is, in certain cases, a sign of great love of truth. Learning to love and trust the other is a strength that has to be acquired."

One sultry afternoon, when Aunt Miriam and I were waiting to be summoned to my mother's room, I asked her what she remembered of Uncle Tullio.

"I remember clearly when I saw him the last time. He was in Paris and we went to the Hôtel Lutetia to say good-bye to him. We were about to emigrate to Zurich, and I

94

know that both my father and my mother had been insisting that Uncle Tullio, Aunt Allegra, and my cousins should join us. My mother begged him to leave Italy, but it was hopeless. My parents had profound respect for Uncle Tullio. They knew he was an idealist, a man of great purity, unlike Uncle Eugenio, whom my parents considered a profiteer."

"In 1943, why did two of Uncle Tullio's sons, who had been in Switzerland, come back to Italy?"

"True, Guido and Giacomo Treves did come to Zurich for a while, but they were younger than I was, and I saw very little of them. I realize it was mad to let them go back to Italy, but at that time I didn't think about it."

"I've heard that Uncle Tullio had a foreign mistress, and the tragedy was her fault."

"It's best to let the dead rest in peace! So many things have been said about poor Uncle Tullio! It's likely that he had a mistress or two, but I doubt there was any question of revenge. Some even say the family's death was collective suicide — that, under Uncle Tullio's influence, they all went and turned themselves in, to get themselves killed and not have to face a different world. All the wicked things you hear come from sinister people, greedy and envious of his money. You mustn't believe gossip. You asked me how I remember him. He was too honest and too upright a man to be understood."

Thüsis told me about her visit to the lawyer, Morpurgo.

"My dear girl," he said to her, "it's odd that a young person like yourself should come and question an old man about a matter that means so much to him, a subject he has talked about a great deal in his own life, but then, as his generation died, has been forgotten. You were quite right to come to me: I knew Tullio Treves well and I can tell you many things about him. He was a physically un-attractive man, with a nasal voice, always yelling, behaving like a miniature Duce; and I despised him because he treated so badly, so cruelly, that marvelous wife of his, Allegra Montalcini. She was beautiful, sweet, extremely sensitive. But it would be pointless and uninteresting for me to go on and on with this kind of memories. Tullio Treves was indeed a Jewish Fascist, but a bad Fascist. He was fanatical about Fascism, but not sincere. He had joined the move-ment to rid himself of certain personal complexes; his spirit was corrupt, weak, and he hid behind an ideology that allowed him to justify his existence and to conceal his inner evil. So he became a fierce activist, a dogged promoter of the Fascist state and, furthermore, a racist, shamefully anti-Semitic. He couldn't accept the fact of being a Jew and he hated everything that reminded him of it. Later, when he was punished by the advent of the racial laws, he let himself go completely, involving himself and his family in tragedy, which, as you know, ended in a massacre. He sought that terrible end himself; he constructed it with his own hands, because he wanted to die and to drag his family with him. When Tullio realized that the war was lost, and was certain they would put him in prison or banish him as an ex-Fascist, he couldn't face such humiliation and preferred to get himself killed, with his whole family, hoping with that martyrdom to sublimate, in the eyes of the world, his squalid life and his bloody past. Only the Germans, not the Fascists, would then be guilty of having slaughtered the innocent. And his own innocence would naturally be enhanced by the fact that a woman and some young chil-dren would be killed with him. Getting himself killed in order to surround himself with a halo of purity and in-nocence was part of his Germanic, Wagnerian ideal. He was so clever in arranging the event that he managed to make people believe that an informer had reported him. Thanks to his money, he had corrupted, fascinated a foreign woman, who for that matter was the mistress of a well-known Fascist. The Fascist, if I'm not mistaken, was later hanged by the partisans. You see, my dear young lady, Baron Treves was a shady individual, and I wouldn't want you to consider him a typical Fascist Jew. I would be doing my coreligionists a disservice, if I allowed you to believe this. Tullio Treves is an isolated case; others, after the advent of Fascism, in the first ten years of the regime, believed Mussolini was a positive force, the man who would stabilize Italy for its own good. But the majority of these people, as soon as the racial laws were issued, either emigrated or gradually forsook the regime. Some took part in the Resistance; others preferred to remain silent."

Both Thüsis and I consider this testimony a verbal settling of scores. In Morpurgo's words there was an exaggerated hate. It isn't possible that Uncle Tullio reported himself and his family to avoid facing the course of history and to pass himself off as a victim. That attitude would reflect an excessive cowardice, which seems to contradict his obstinacy and a certain reckless courage he had.

We've discovered that Esther Moscati is still alive and living in Turin. We went to see her, with the story that we were the American niece and nephew of Uncle Tullio and we had heard how close she was to him in the terrible days before his death.

Signorina Moscati agreed to receive us, in her little apartment in via Pio V, not far from the synagogue.

She was an elderly woman, frail-looking and very refined. She had a sweet smile, and after asking us to be seated, she said immediately: "I remember that Baron Treves had a brother living in America, but he didn't like to talk about him."

"Yes, there were some little differences between our grandfather and our uncle; and unfortunately at home any talk about Uncle Tullio and his family was always evasive. They say he was very much involved with the Fascist regime, that he led a very stormy love life, but we haven't come to see you in order to ask about gossip. We were curious to meet someone who unquestionably shared supremely important moments with him and who can perhaps tell us the truth about how he was killed. We were told that Uncle Tullio was betrayed by a foreign woman, the mistress of a famous Fascist. She supposedly also reported our aunt and our cousins. In a diary our uncle kept we came on your name a number of times. References like, 'If it were not for that saint, Esther . . .' "

Naturally Signorina Moscati was moved by these words of Thüsis, who was revealing an extraordinary skill at telling lies.

"I feel honored, to discover after all these years that Baron Treves had such respect for me. I was only a domestic. Working for him was unforgettable, and even today, when I think of his tragic end, I can't help crying. When the baron hired me, in corso Vittorio, I thought he was a bachelor; I didn't know about the baronessa Treves and the children. It was only when I learned about them that I realized Signora Céleste had been the one to report them. Perhaps after some jealous scene, or in a state of intoxication. They drank a great deal of champagne: the lady would bring it. She must have gone and reported him to the German authorities. Not that she was an evil woman; with me, on certain occasions, she was generous. But she was moody and unpredictable, and when she was in one of her raving fits, she would do anything. For example, I learned from the baron that she had several times tried to kill herself."

"Are you sure it was Signora Céleste who reported him? Do you think she's still alive? Why didn't you later report that woman, if you're sure she was the one who handed Uncle and his family over to the Nazis?"

"In all the confusion at the end of the war, she must have found a safe refuge somewhere; rich people always save themselves. And she had contacts everywhere. I'm convinced she was the one who turned them in, but she did it without thinking, in a moment of jealousy. I never revealed my suspicions because I had no proof, and I wouldn't have known how to trace her."

Seeing that Signorina Moscati was becoming agitated, feeling that Thüsis was accusing her of having done nothing to unmask Céleste, I intervened, saying: "To be sure, it would have been impossible for you to make an accusation. It would be interesting to know what became of that woman, and perhaps find her and talk to her. If nothing happened to her and, as you imagine, she got away safely at the end of the war, do you think she would still be alive, or would she be too old?"

"She could be alive. I think she was more or less my age."

I went on: "When you talk about jealousy and betrayal, do you think the signora was jealous of you? Did she suspect that between you and Uncle Tullio there was an intimate relationship?"

"Why, what are you saying! She was jealous of Baronessa Allegra and the children. Mind you, I was very different then from what I am now; I was an attractive girl, but there couldn't have been anything like that."

Then Thüsis spoke up again, seeing that Signorina Moscati had calmed down and was talking more willingly.

"But why was she jealous of the family? You see, we've always been told that Uncle Tullio was an odd man. Weren't there other reasons?"

"Now that I think about it, it's possible that some of the baron's oddities may have irritated the signora Céleste. But so many years have gone by, I really couldn't say. I recall they had a number of arguments about the costume trunk."

Thüsis and I asked at the same time: "What was the costume trunk?"

"Oh, of course, you couldn't know, and perhaps I shouldn't talk about it, but really it was harmless; he only did it when he was tired. In a big trunk he kept some women's clothes, and on some evenings, when he was alone, he would turn the gramophone up as loud as it would go, military marches or German operas, and he would dress up as a woman of some specific period — often they were old and valuable dresses — and he would have me wait on him at table. He wanted me to call him signora baronessa, then he would shut himself up in his bedroom and listen to music, and I could hear him moving around the room. Perhaps he was dancing by himself. You see, there was no harm in any of it; but when Signora Céleste discovered the trunk there were terrible yells; she immediately thought the dresses belonged to another woman."

I could not help asking: "Then she reported him because of the trunk!"

"No, she did that quite a while afterward. The trunk vanished right after the scene. The baron swore the dresses were his mother's; she called him a liar, but the whole question was shelved. The baron told me to hide some other dresses in a wardrobe, and for a little while he went on with his usual solitary ritual, with my help. But then the real drama exploded, I think it was late winter in 1943, when she arrived unexpectedly and caught the baron, in woman's clothes, dancing with a pillow in his arms, in the bedroom, sprinkled with perfume. Tuberose. It's still a mystery to me, how he managed to get hold of those bottles of perfume. . . . I think that scene was what made Signora Céleste's suspicions become certainties; she kept accusing him of being a homosexual. Blind with jealousy, she pretended not to understand that, being a special person, the baron needed some distraction in those horrible moments, even if it did take such an eccentric form. But I think that, after that evening, she felt a kind of frustration."

"Hence the definite accusation of homosexuality and the suspicion that you were his accomplice."

"But I told you: they were just moments of relaxation."

"But we know he was a homosexual, and nobody in the family denies it. Today it would be ridiculous to try to hide it."

"I understand, but now I feel guilty. I let myself be carried away, telling you some details that cast a shadow on him. The baron would have died anyway, even if the signora hadn't turned him in. How could a man like that reconstruct a life for himself? His wife, Baronessa Allegra, had become unrecognizable, depressed, moody, after they lost their first son, who died of typhus. You can't understand, because you weren't even born then, how reacting with frivolity, with eccentric behavior could be excusable in those days, considering how exhausting and precarious everything was. It was just another way for the baron, even in Fascism's defeat, to express that Fascist slogan 'me ne frego,' I don't give a damn. He was profaning the world, by dressing up. It was just another way of rebelling against a disgusting time when everybody, and especially us Jews, was totally impotent."

"In other words, his dressing up was also symbolic."

"That's how I came to think of it, as the years went by. I worked as a maid because I wasn't allowed to attend drama school. Afterward it was too late, and I was never able to fulfill myself in life. We played roles, to escape from those nights of fear and cold. Living with the fear that anyone might come in and arrest us . . ."

Thüsis said, "Excuse me, Signorina Moscati, it might seem that we came to interrogate you. We just meant to pay a visit, and then the questions came spontaneously, out of curiosity."

"I understand that."

"I wanted to ask you if that woman was beautiful and if the two of them were really in love."

"I believe they were very much in love. She reported him because she loved him, and I believe that he, too, in his way, was fascinated. I'm convinced he was fascinated to know that an Aryan woman, a foreigner, openly attached to a well-known Fascist official, was in love with him. It was a revenge against his cruel fate. I can't say that Signora Céleste was ugly; perhaps she looked older than she was, and her skin wasn't beautiful. I remember she had dark blue eyes, was always tanned; her hair was blond and silky, but the striking thing about her was her bearing, a bearing that wasn't normal then and wouldn't exist today . . ."

13

My mother's funeral was held yesterday; she died on Sunday, at three in the afternoon. Aunt Elvira and Aunt Miriam were with her. Grandfather Dimitri and I had been to see her before lunch. Though she was very ill, and though we were prepared, nobody imagined she would die like that. We were expecting a sign, an indication of her worsening, a heartbreaking scream. Instead, she died while she was talking with my aunts. She went off, staring into the void. We are all overwhelmed. We had become used to the fact that she was dying, but it seemed as if that condition, her being incurably ill, should last forever. And so every time I went in to see her I had the feeling that we would see each other again. This doesn't mean that I had any hope of a cure, but I knew she was there, in bed, well cared for, in a kind of constant doze, like a dream. I lived with Thüsis, I thought of the exploits of Tullio and Céleste, I came and went between city and country. Now she is gone; there will be no more visits, no more aunts. All of them will go back to their houses, and I will be left the possessions and the memories of my mother. For my grandfather Dimitri, too, it seems impossible that she is dead.

A few minutes after her death she seemed to me tinier, no longer a person, but a precious object within which the blood had ceased to throb, and on her face, the suffering, the marks of her struggle to live were transformed into sweetness, serenity . . . That body from which my mother's soul was separated was now only the form of a silent and modest woman who, all the same, had given me life. Everything said about death is surely banal, but it is strange how we, the living, see it. For example, the day before yesterday, I noted that Grandfather was observing with great attention every single movement of the man sealing the coffin with a blowtorch. He watched with the eye of someone aware it will soon be his turn. His gaze showed no sign of sadness, only curiosity.

The funeral began at two in the afternoon, under a blazing sun. A rabbi came, middle-aged, wearing a black hat, and acting as if he were in a hurry to get the ceremony over with as soon as possible so that he could then go on to more interesting concerns. This rabbi must consider himself a great philosopher, and so he performed this funeral ceremony with detachment. He seemed to want to make sure that all of us present understood his job wasn't digging graves, and this was only one of the many unpleasant tasks imposed upon him by an ill-educated society, unable to recognize his exceptional gifts as a thinker. So he had come to perform his job and make us pay for his vainglory. The moment the coffin was set in place and closed alongside those of my father and grandparents, the rabbi took his leave, with detached respect; he nodded to some members of the family, then left.

At the cemetery, too, my grandfather Dimitri continued to observe with great attention that rite, probably wondering what would be the season of his death and the hour of his burial. Among those present, some were in tears; others assumed the sober mien of those who suffer in silence.

I have remained alone in the villa; the others are all gone, and now this has become my house. What will happen to me? Will I have to give up my studio in London and come to live in Turin? Thüsis has gone to Corsica and wants me to join her there. Grandfather Dimitri also suggested I take a little holiday with Thüsis, before I start thinking about what my future will be. These days I have seemed to live in what I imagine the cosmic void must be. No past, no future; mist, lack of any center of gravity. My life seems a terrible weight, unbearable; and at the same time everything I have done seems light and ephemeral. On the very day of my mother's death, a notary read her will, which said that I am the sole heir of all her possessions. It would be useless to describe the horrified look in the eyes of the various relatives present, who were expecting something. To dispel the grouchiness and to get rid of them, I immediately told all the people who had been living in the villa and tending my mother to select some object in her memory.

To be sure, it's not easy for me to take in the fact that I am an orphan, that I have inherited a fortune and, with it, burdensome responsibilities. After my mother's death, instead of being a penniless youth, I have suddenly become a rich man. I could live in grand hotels, buy a Rolls-Royce! I saw myself heaping up gold ingots, burning banknotes; holding piles and piles of dollars in my hand and seeing them move to the hands of others, as I buy things. This situation frightens me a little. With Cinderella, it would have strengthened my position, but with Thüsis it could become a problem: I'll have to be very careful not to outrage her sensibilities and not to change our life. And so, following my grandfather Dimitri's advice, I'll go and join her in Corsica. There I'll meet Uncle Bill, who is apparently a fascinating man, with many ex-wives, who commutes between Ajaccio and New York. We will be able to make him tell us what he knows of Céleste.

Before joining Thüsis in Ajaccio, I had to stop off in Paris. Both Grandfather and Aunt Miriam insisted I should go and speak as soon as possible with Rosenberg, an international tax expert, to get his advice about various questions connected with my inheritance.

For the first time in my life I stayed at the Ritz, where I couldn't resist the temptation of calling Cinderella in London. A very polite gentleman answered, telling me that Cinderella was in Paris, at the Meurice. I called her at once, and she agreed to have supper with me. I was curious to see her reaction to the change in my life. Naturally she didn't react as I had imagined. She found it quite normal that I should be at the Ritz, normal to eat at my expense in the garden of a famous restaurant, normal to be driven around Paris in a black limousine . . .

All through supper she did nothing but talk of trivialities; she asked me nothing about my mother, or about Thüsis, she never mentioned her children or her former husband.

The conversation shifted from the beauty of Paris gardens to a Monet show where her interest had been aroused by a painting of bullfighting, which had made her homesick for Spain and thus for a summer on Ibiza. Then, unexpectedly, in a stern voice, she said to me: "I found some notes of yours in a drawer at home. How far have you got with the novel? I have the feeling you're spreading yourself thin, not working much. You should write more, the way you did in London. Are you still engaged?"

"I believe I'm in love with Thüsis."

"I'd like you to take me to some little hotel. This torrid heat arouses me. I adore this pale sky, this milky sun, this thick, humid air. There doesn't seem to be a breath of wind. I'd like us to get out of the car and take the métro. We'd get off when we were too sweaty and tired, then we'd go . . ."

We ended up in a little hotel around Saint-Denis, where the heat was murderous. Looking out of the window, you could see nothing but other people distraught by the sultriness, keeping their windows opened wide, in the illusion of fighting the heat with a breath of air, using books as fans, and talking only of the heat and how uncomfortable it was. At eleven, Cinderella asked me to take her to the Old Navy, a bar on boulevard Saint-Germain.

"A lot of old foreign journalists go there. There are little jukeboxes at the tables. I want to hear some French rock and eat a croque-monsieur."

Around midnight Cinderella said to me: "Take me back to my hotel; I have to leave at the crack of dawn."

She didn't want me to come up with her and we said goodbye hastily, with a touch of shyness and melancholy. At the Ritz, I thought for a long time, wondering whether I should call her, start it all over again; but in the end I didn't, and I spent the sleepless night looking at the plaster decorations on the ceiling. I felt like a child, in that mood when they say 'I want my mama,' and I thought how I would never see mine again. Tall, very thin, with her short gray hair, pale and sweet eyes. Cinderella, in any case, was not the woman of my life, and I was no longer in love with her. It seemed to me that those games, always the same, made up of little, constant provocations, were silly, empty as soap bubbles. Cinderella toyed with me, releasing in our games all her repressed desires.

Thüsis was much more fascinating; but with her, too, I didn't know what would happen. We had to get to know each other better. I didn't even know if she had other men. The one certitude for us was our sexual relationship. Thüsis had attracted me from the day I saw her in the Pensione Europa.

That night at the Ritz, I also decided I would ask her to marry me. I remembered a time when I was about to marry Anna, and a cousin of mine asked me: "Why are you two getting married? What's the point? What difference does it make?"

When I tried to explain to that boy the reasons why I wanted to marry Anna, I stammered. Then I asked myself: Why does anyone write a book? Why have children? It's an instinct. I wouldn't have wanted to marry Cinderella, but Thüsis, yes. Aunt Miriam and Grandfather would be pleased. Now I have to talk to her about it. Maybe I'm being conceited, and she will say she doesn't want me, that she's too young, and that she's against marriage . . .

PART FIVE

Corsica

14

Thüsis came to meet me at the airport. I saw her from a distance. She was impatiently smoking, pacing up and down, her arms behind her back, one foot flung out. Her hair was bound by a rubber band; she had on a T-shirt with "Coca-Cola" printed on it, and a pair of floppy men's shorts. She gave me a hasty kiss and said: "Couldn't you travel with a carry-on bag? The plane was already half an hour late, and Uncle Bill's waiting for us in Ajaccio. For tonight I couldn't say no to him, so we're having supper at their place, but it's the first and last time. They really are a pain in the ass with all their snobbishness! And Nancy, after seven o'clock, is always smashed."

We climbed into an ancient, pale-blue Cadillac with white-wall tires. Inside, it was all plastic, again in pastels; and Thüsis grabbed the white Bakelite wheel as if it were a rudder and she were the captain of a ship. She handled that blue whale like a bicycle, driving barefoot and lighting one cigarette after another.

The traffic was terrible; she huffed.

I felt drab, unwanted, and I regretted being there. I didn't appreciate that curt, indifferent treatment. And how I wished the girl didn't smoke so much!

"Kiss me. I want you."

I heard that voice through the traffic. She had grasped my hand — it was a red light; and she put her lips to mine. We kissed until we irritated the man in the car behind us, who started honking furiously, and then many others behind him; the noise soon became infernal.

Thüsis, starting the blue car again, remarked: "Hot blood around here! This was Daffy's car, and now it's mine, like everything else. This is the first time I've come back to Corsica since he died, and I see only him in everything I do. I must say that Uncle Bill is very sweet with me, but he doesn't realize that I find his sweetness exasperating because it just makes me miss Daffy all the more. Uncle Bill's chatter and gossip make me long for my father's often unpleasant words. When you see the houses, you'll understand everything. We have some land twenty-five kilometers from here; I'll take you there this evening. On the estate there's a luxurious villa complete with swimming pool; and Uncle Bill lives with Nancy, his sixth wife, and there's a shepherd's house on the tip of a promontory, where you have to draw water from a well, and there's no electricity or telephone. That's where Daffy lived, and now it's my house. The property is divided in two by a little wall. You'll see: it's impossible not to tell planned, refined gardens from rank Mediterranean brush. In Ajaccio there are two boats, the *Thüsis,* a sailboat that's now mine, and Uncle Bill's motorboat, naturally renamed *Nancy.*"

"And did Bill tell you if you have an aunt named Céleste and if she's still alive?"

"Yes. So, you see, I wasn't mistaken. Her name is Céleste, and she lives in New York. I realize he's embarrassed by her, and he'd rather not talk about her with me. So I brought up the subject by saying that you were about to arrive, and you're a historian who specializes in the Fascist period, and you would like to ask him some questions about our aunt who, if I had it right, was a last-ditch Fascist."

"Now I'm the one who has to talk to him about Aunt Céleste?"

"That's right. I'll lead up to it, but, since she's alive and, according to Uncle Bill, lives in New York, I believe the most interesting thing would be to go and see her as soon as possible. Here we are. You see that café on the corner with the blue-and-yellow-striped awnings? The Café Ajaccio? You see that gray-haired gentleman dressed in white linen?"

"Yes."

"That's Bill."

"Why on earth is he wearing a jacket and tie?"

"That's the custom here, when you come into the city. Daffy used to do the same thing. Except he always wore dark blue. And a black tie. They are *sgiò*. I suppose you would say gentlemen; in Corsica they're considered local lords. And landowners here wear jacket and tie. It's the custom."

We parked the blue whale and walked up an avenue flanked with palm trees, the sidewalk covered with blue and yellowish tiles. The same colors, slightly faded, are to be seen on the shutters of the local houses. At the café, on every table I saw a carafe of water and some glasses of Pastis.

Bill was a tall man, thin and tanned. He spoke to us in English, taking it for granted that I knew the language, and this was the first time I heard Thüsis speak like an American. He said to me immediately: "I hear you're a historian. I hope you like it here on our island. Nancy's waiting for us at home. Now we'll have a drink, while the rush hour passes, and then we'll go. Have you come from Paris?"

"Yes."

"How was the weather? Was the city crowded?"

"The heat was awful, and the city seemed deserted. Nobody in the streets, many shops closed."

"I haven't been in Paris during the summer for years and years; now I just pass through on my way from New York. I think the city's become boring and expensive. In the old days you could live there on nothing, there were lots of artists, it was fun. It was pretty much the way Hemingway described it; but now there are awful people."

Thüsis was a bit irritated by her uncle's sociable joviality. I realized she would have liked her father to be in his place — in a dark suit, surly, rude, treating her like a man. In the car Uncle Bill went on talking, asking me questions. Thüsis drove in silence, very fast, jerkily, slamming on the brakes when she wanted to punish her talkative uncle for not having died instead of her father. Actually, if it hadn't been for Daffy's immanent ghost, I would have warmed to this American gentleman who was telling me all about Corsica in a forced Oxford accent.

Nancy appeared in the doorway: typical American woman of a certain age, too much in every way. Too much makeup, too much politeness and affectation, too keyed up . . .

It would be pointless to describe Thüsis's growing impatience, my embarrassment, and the inexhaustible jollity of the couple. I didn't dare bring up the subject of Aunt Céleste, because I realized Thüsis wanted us to leave as soon as possible. In fact, shortly after the meal was over, she said: "Alberto Claudio is very tired. It was sweet of you to invite us, but now we must be going . . ."

"I thought you said Alberto Claudio wanted to talk with me?" Bill said, taken by surprise.

"Yes, but there'll be time. We're nearby."

Nancy said, "We won't disturb you, because we can imagine you want to be left alone; but consider yourselves invited whenever you want to come. We'll be happy to see you!"

Uncle Bill added: "Darling, are you sure you don't want me to send Maria over?"

"No, thanks. Good night, Uncle Bill. Good night, Nancy."

Finally we were free, and I no longer was embarrassed by Thüsis's constant sighs, the click of her Zippo, and the way she raised her eyes to heaven. We reached Daffy's house on the tip of the promontory. The house is as simple as a Franciscan monastery, in the midst of nature. From the terrace you see the moon and the sea.

"Now aren't the houses different?"

"Yes."

"I'll take you to Daffy's room. I want you to sleep there."

"But, actually, I'd like to sleep with you."

"That's impossible here. There are two rooms, mine and Daffy's; and there is just one army cot in each. The rooms were conceived as tents, on an expedition."

"Couldn't we find a mattress, make ourselves a bed?"

"No, I don't want the habits of this place to change. I'm surprised you don't understand that this is a proof of love. You mustn't think I would allow just anyone to sleep in my father's room. Come on!"

It was a whitewashed room, with a cot under a pale blue linen cover, a table, a chair, a wardrobe of blond wood, and a few books on some shelves. Over the bed there was an abstract painting, undoubtedly the work of Uncle Bill. I had seen a number of his pictures at his villa. Strangely, this talkative man never spoke of his work.

Opposite the table there was a great, open window and the moon and the sea were visible, as from the terrace. The table was bare.

"You like it? My room's the same, only I don't have the view of the sea. Come, I'll show it to you."

In fact, the furnishings were the same, only there was a bit of disorder: a suitcase on the floor, clothes on the chair, and a number of papers on the writing table. In Thüsis's room there were no paintings; only a poster, a Picasso Pierrot. The rest of the house comprised the kitchen and a sitting room.

"If you want to wash, you fill the bucket at the well, then in the kitchen you can take the pitcher and basin that belonged to Daffy. If you're not tired, we could go to the point and look at the sea. My father and I always did that after supper. We would look at the sea without saying anything."

As I struggled through the brush, Thüsis walked over the pebbles barefoot, and I kept thinking how she had changed. In this place she seemed haunted, and I thought she wanted to bring her father back to life through me. I felt myself observed, judged, as if she wanted me to play a part.

I had to put a quick end to this misunderstanding that was beginning to torment me. "You know, I thought about you, in Paris, about us; and I wanted to talk to you."

"But we'll keep quiet now for a bit, all right? You'll see how beautiful it is to look at the sea, in silence."

I found her overbearing, and I had no desire to look at that dark sea or at that too-bright moon. And it was obviously impossible to contemplate the sea in silence, since the crickets were all crying.

When we were back at the house, Thüsis showed me the well and gave me a piece of soap. In the kitchen I tried to kiss her, and I asked her: "Want me to come to your room for a while? For one reason or another we've been separated too many nights."

"No. Not tonight. This is the first time I've been in this house with another person."

"But it's important for you to forget the past! I understand your grief, but Daffy is gone now, and we have to think of our life. Don't you want to have a child?"

"I don't want to talk about it now. Try to understand me, and forgive me if I seem a bit strange. Tomorrow it will be better, just wait."

"I want you. If you like, we can go somewhere else. Why don't we make love in the garden, in the moonlight?"

"I thought I had made it clear: this evening the answer is no. Can't you understand?"

Hurt, I withdrew to my room. After all, I was the one who had just lost his mother, and she hadn't uttered one word of condolence. I had arrived in Corsica only a few hours before, and already I was feeling too many negative vibrations . . . While I was lying on the bed, thinking of the disastrous situation I had ended up in, fortunately I heard the footsteps of Thüsis, who came into the room, sat on the bed, and caressed me.

"Alberto Claudio, don't be angry with me, don't believe that I'm looking to you as a replacement for Daffy. I love you, I love this room, and I'm glad you're the first man to sleep in this bed after his death. Daffy was very important for me, and here, among this brush, in this simplicity, this silence, is the one place I've been able to find myself again. I'd like you to become fond of this room, which has a very special, symbolic meaning for me. I always envied my father because he had a window overlooking the sea. He used to write and smoke there, facing the sea; and if I wanted to come in, I had to knock. Since this can never become my room, I've taken everything from this desk, and I want it to become yours. I want to initiate you into my old rituals here. I want you to get to know this nature that lives inside me even when I'm traveling around the world and feel torn. And I want to introduce you to Vinicio, our sailor, and if you don't know Corsica, I'd like to take you on the boat as far as Bonifacio. And now good night, sleep well; I'll come and wake you."

"But do you still love me?"

"Yes."

"How much?"

"More all the time."

"Would you like to marry me?"

"We'll see; first we have to know each other better. Tomorrow I want to talk to you about Aunt Céleste. Good night."

"Good night to you, too. Will you give me a kiss?"

She did, on the forehead, and she went out of the room, leaving the door ajar. My earlier irritation and anger were turned into sweetness. Suddenly I found this room beautiful, as it had become mine. I knew now a different facet of Thüsis: her love of nature, her respect for certain rituals. She possessed great strength and courage, and I was curious to be guided through the maze of that hermit existence of earth and sea where, almost like a plant, she felt she had her roots.

Waking, I heard a voice singing softly, and I called out: "Thüsis, where are you?"

"In the kitchen. I'm making coffee. It's eleven. Want some bread, butter, and honey?"

"Yes, thanks, I'll be right down."

In the bedroom there were no curtains, and there, through

the window where I had seen the moon, I could now see the sun, already high.

While we were peacefully having breakfast on a stone table in front of the house, shaded by a fig tree, we heard the sound of Uncle Bill's voice.

"I wanted to find out how our young guest is. Did he sleep well? Do you two want to come out on the boat with us?"

"No, thank you, Uncle Bill."

"Will you come to supper then?"

"No, thanks."

"For a drink, at least. I have to talk with Alberto Claudio about Céleste."

"Yes, Uncle Bill, we'll talk about her."

"I think the picture in your brother's room is very interesting," I said, without thinking.

"You know abstract painting?"

"Well, a bit. I think your work is good."

"Come and see me this afternoon, then. I'll show you my studio, and we can talk about painting. Will you bring him, Thüsis?"

"We'll see. I have other plans today, and now Alberto Claudio and I have to go into town. Have a nice outing!"

"Thanks, I'll expect you in the late afternoon."

Thüsis turned toward me, irked, and said, as she lit a cigarette: "Why did you have to talk to him about his painting? Now we'll have to pay homage to the great artist!"

"Sorry, I was just being polite."

"I can't bear that couple another moment. Tomorrow I'm going to take you out on the boat; they'll have to leave us in peace then at least. You go see the studio on your own: get him to tell you about Céleste. It's unbelievable! When Daffy was here, Bill would never have dared. He and those damned whores of his, and his stories, and his drinks . . . "

15

Thüsis's moods have grown worse. In spite of her hostile, downright rude manner, we haven't ever managed to shake off the honeyed politeness of Nancy and Bill, who keep trying, morning and evening, to invite us over, to introduce us to some "charming people." I have also begun to find them tiresome, and especially Nancy, extremely boring with that way she has of talking aggressive nonsense already with her second martini.

Bill's pictures are fairly decorative and therefore easy to sell for vacation houses, banks, offices. Abstract paintings, in good taste, but, as far as I can see, without any creative commitment or thrust. His paintings are the mirror of his life and his behavior.

When I asked him about Céleste and the war, Bill told me he didn't know much. She is now very old, lives in New York, where they see each other as rarely as possible.

"She's a tormented woman, who destroys everything she touches. I don't mean to say she has the evil eye, but surely she's driven by an evil force. Besides, I've never liked her, because she always preferred my brother; she only kept up relations with him, actually. In any case, if you come to New York, as I hope you will, I'll see that you meet her. Here on Corsica they know her well at Corte, the ancient capital of the island, where we have a family home that served her as a refuge during the de-Nazification period. Daffy was the one who hid her."

Bill also tried to establish some complicity between us, hinting that Thüsis was too reserved and antisocial and that, in her own interest, I should try to make her more outgoing.

The day after my visit to Uncle Bill's studio, Thüsis announced: "Tomorrow we're sailing to Bonifacio. I've spoken with Vinicio, the sea is good, and the forecast is favorable. We're going fishing. I think a change of air will do us both good."

In the Ajaccio harbor we boarded the *Thüsis*, a sailboat with a dark hull and a deck of unpainted wood.

Vinicio is a man about fifty, thin, taciturn. He and Thüsis speak in sign language. We sailed all day long, and at nightfall we cast our nets. We caught some sea scorpions and bream, which we baked in foil. Vinicio was the real captain on board, and though I often heard him refer to "*sgiò* Daffy," and "Monsieur Daffy," and what he used to say and used to do, Daffy's presence was felt less heavily than in the house. And further, we had left uncle and aunt behind, and I could sense that Thüsis was happier.

We sailed and fished for three days. Then we arrived at the Strait of Bonifacio, a really impressive sight. The town, on a desolate peak above that enormous promontory, has great fascination. At the tip of the promontory there is the headquarters of the Foreign Legion. It is hard to imagine a more fitting seat for that adventurers' and mercenaries' army.

After our visit to Bonifacio, Thüsis's mood has definitely changed. The Spartan life of the sea and the fishing were good for her. At night we drank cognac or rum and then, when we thought Vinicio was otherwise occupied, we made love in haste, still dressed. Our bodies were salty and baked by the sun.

I told Thüsis I would have to go back to Turin in a week. She couldn't come with me because first she had to deal with the sale of a farm in the Calenzana area. Besides, she had to talk with her uncle because she wanted to eliminate as much jointly held property as she could. They would own together only the big house at Corte.

"These few days that are left: what if we made a trip in the car?"

"We could go toward Corte, see our house, and then go on to Calvi."

So we went back to Ajaccio, collected the blue Cadillac to go to Corte.

There we stopped at a café, where the proprietress, a stout woman with flabby cheeks and watery eyes, a Gauloise without filter dangling from her moist lips, served us two sandwiches of blackbird pâté and some beer.

An elderly man was seated by the jukebox, dressed in black, completely concentrated on the crossword puzzle in *Corse Matin*. Then he started looking hard at Thüsis and finally, unable to restrain himself, he spoke to her: "Forgive me for taking the liberty, but are you by any chance a member of the Foulk family?"

"Yes, I am. Why?"

"This is extraordinary! You must be the daughter of Daffy. Am I right?"

"Yes, I'm his daughter."

"Poor man, he died far away, and they didn't bury him here. I knew him from the time he was a boy. I'm the pastor of the Corte diocese. When he used to come to Corte, I would go and have dinner with him in the family palace, and he always talked to me about you. I would never have believed there could be such a resemblance."

"You think I look like my father?"

"Yes, a bit, also, but, if I may say so, you're the living image of your great-aunt Céleste when she was your age. Céleste is a remarkable woman: the kind you don't run into anymore. She lived here in Corte almost a year, we saw each other every day: it was just after the end of the war. Forgive me for talking to you like this about her, but the two of you resemble each other in a striking way. I'm sure any number of people must have told you that, and in New York I daresay you see her often."

"No, I don't know her. I live in Italy, and though I've often heard her spoken of, nobody ever told me I look like her."

"You're identical. If you don't know her, you should go and see her in the States. Unfortunately, it's been years since she visited these parts, but we write each other always at Christmas, and in every letter she tells me she wants to be buried here at Corte with her brother and her parents. For her the place where you rest forever is always your true home; the one you must choose, because that's where our body will stay, and it's the only place where the living can come and visit us."

"You know, it's very strange that you should talk to me about my aunt Céleste, because I am very curious about her; there are all sorts of things I want to know. She's a mysterious figure, full of shadows. I know she was involved with the Fascist regime and had many love affairs, but I can't understand if she is really extraordinary, as many people describe her, or a monster, as others say."

"Here at Corte, it's true, there are those who consider her perverse, because she was committed to Fascism, and because she had various lovers at that time, including a Jew in Turin! The fact that she sincerely believed in a totalitarian regime — and I'm sure she never changed her ideas — is not a sin; it's an ideology, like any other; and the fact that she had love affairs, though I'm a priest and believe in the sacrament of matrimony, doesn't prevent me from assuring you that your aunt is a person of great moral qualities. She's a woman capable of unusual outbursts of generosity, capable of renunciation, of making sacrifices. I can't tell you how, even today, I still look back with nostalgia on those months she spent in our city, those evenings when we would have supper together and talk for hours. Céleste knows well both our language and our mentality. She has always felt, in herself, the free spirit of us Corsicans. She fell in love with a Jew, and even if he was banned and condemned by the Nazi-Fascists like herself, she loved him to the end. When she found out that they had killed that man and his family, it was a terrible drama for her. She even felt remorse for having been, in some way, responsible for that misfortune."

I don't know why, but I was irritated by that priest's ugly mouth, the thick lips, too pink and twisted; and I disliked all his talk of "Corsicans" and "Jews" and "Fascists"; his determination to link Thüsis and Céleste as closely as possible. I interrupted him curtly, and asked: "You express yourself very well in Italian. How is that?"

"Ah, I know Italy well; I lived a long time in Leghorn, and I still have many friends there. Now that's a place where you really eat well."

We spent two days shut up in the family palazzo, lying in a great canopied baroque bed, and enjoying the service of an old domestic who constantly brought us bottles of wine, mountain salami, bread, and cakes. We laughed till we cried in that huge grim building, where Thüsis insisted there was a ghost. I waited until we were in Calvi, the last stop on our trip around Corsica, to speak of Céleste and of a trip to New York.

"If we go to New York we could get married and live there. I like living in countries where they speak English."

"This winter we'll enjoy living in Turin, too; wait and see. It's interesting, protective to live in that city full of cafés and arcades, where the people always seem indifferent."

"I don't know, I feel terribly sad when I think how that empty villa and that estate belong to me, and now I have to go back there, and pay visits to farms and rice fields. . . . I wish somebody would free me from everything and I could escape to Australia or Argentina. Or no, Greece. Escape to Greece and find a white house there, olives, the sea, a bit like here . . ."

"Then we could stay here?"

"No, you have too many memories, too many roots. Memories of childhood, the places where you saw loved ones live and then die, are sad. Moving where our family moved, without them, discovering a trace of them in every plate, every blanket, every room. Memory should be something you carry inside yourself, something that surfaces, unexpected, sudden, you can't say when. I can't live surrounded by memories; it's as if they were stifling me."

"I understand you. I would also like to remember Corsica, but free myself of all the things I have here. It used to happen to me often, there in Turin. I would be walking under the arcades from the pension to class, it would be raining and gloomy, and I would see the blue water, the reddish cliffs baked by the sun and lashed by the wind and sea. I'm a woman of the sea. Only the sea gives me life: that tang, that sound, the constant flux and reflux. The slamming of the waves, the winds, the sails."

During that automobile trip, between me and Thüsis a

spontaneous friendship was established, beyond our love; and for the first time we managed to communicate freely.

Thüsis talked to me about what dance meant in her life, and I told her how I wanted to find the time to write a novel.

At this point my departure was imminent, and I found myself looking at the sea as if for the last ime. Actually, I was sensing that twilight atmosphere that hangs over the last days of August when you feel summer fading. I have always felt a horror of four o'clock on a winter afternoon. The sunset hour arrives too early; it seems evening, when it's really afternoon. In other words, I felt that sadness that precedes departure and end of season. On my last day it was impossible to get out of a farewell supper at Uncle Bill's.

When we arrived, Nancy was already drunk, and Bill was particularly jolly and talkative. They asked us a thousand questions about our cruise and our trip in the car, but the questions were so long that they implied no answer was necessary. As soon as Thüsis said, "We went to Bonifacio," Bill said, "You don't mean to tell me, darling, that you went all the way there just with Vinicio. I can imagine how he grumbled! And I know without asking that you caught bream and then more bream, and you took Alberto Claudio to eat in the harbor at the restaurant where poor Daffy always used to go."

During the night Thüsis came into my bed, and afterward she wanted us to go out among the brush and look at the moon, but dawn was almost breaking.

As she drove the Cadillac toward the airport, Thüsis was sad and silent. I told her not to worry, that we would soon be together again.

She asked me: "You feel contempt for me, don't you?"

"Why?"

"Because I profaned my father's room. And you didn't have the same pleasure as usual, either."

"That's not true. Ever since we've been together in Corsica, I've felt we love each other in a more complete way. It's beautiful when an erotic and violent relationship is also sometimes sentimental and sweet. And as for the room, didn't you say it had become mine?"

"Well then, if it seems to you that we're so much in love, why didn't you ask me to leave with you?"

"Thüsis, you know very well I didn't ask you because you can't come! Do you think it's fun for me to go off alone to that gloomy villa, full of memories, to talk about money, property . . ."

"What do you think I'm doing here?"

"Let's hope this period doesn't last long. Are you still in love with me?"

"Yes, very much."

"How much?"

"This much."

"Not enough."

"Then even more, but you mustn't take advantage."

I left Corsica, thinking that ours was a great love, and already as I was boarding the plane, I felt homesick for those places, the days spent there. That island had become part of me, with its climate, its landscape, its smells. Seaside villages and country towns; shepherds, sailors, peasants . . .

PART SIX

Rapachi:
The Secret Notebook

16

Going back to the villa was worse than I had imagined. I think almost constantly of Thüsis and of our holiday on Corsica, while my days are filled with meetings with lawyers, accountants, farmers, who talk to me only of money and responsibilities. All I hear is that now that it all belongs to me, I must pay attention to this or that, trust this man, distrust that other, all of them people I don't know. I have no idea how I can escape this situation.

The evenings are long and lugubrious. My only break is the phone call of Thüsis, who calls me from a public booth between eight and nine. After supper I roam around this immense house where once a lot of people lived, you could hear children's shouts and laughter; and now I'm the only one here. Our family home is laden with stories and anecdotes, I know it would be immoral to sell it, but owning it, like so many other things my mother left me, fills me with anguish. Feeling myself bound to lands and places, only because they're mine, unable to get rid of them because it's not done, because I have a child who one day might . . .

The thing that impresses me most is that Uncle Tullio spent his childhood and adolescence here, and then lived here with Aunt Allegra and their children. I often wonder what he would be like if he were still alive. At certain moments I feel contempt for him; at others, affection. Then I am gripped by the desire to leave for New York, to go and talk with Céleste. She knows everything about him and is the only one who knows the truth. But what's the point of finding out if she was a police informer? By now it isn't so much discovering the truth about the Treves business that interests me; after all this reading, pondering, questioning, I seem to know them, both Tullio and Céleste, with the difference that he is dead and she is still alive.

It's strange how, as I wander through the rooms of this house, I feel the presence of Uncle Tullio.

The walls where I live enclose secrets that I could discover. My curiosity isn't an eagerness to know whether my relatives were right or wrong to keep the story a secret. The fact is that I feel the man is so alive and present that I wonder if, also between us, there aren't resemblances like those the old priest at Corte said existed between Céleste and Thüsis.

These past few days, on a number of occasions, in the kitchen, the garden, the farmyard, I've seen Rapachi moving about, an old farmer; and I've been thinking that he must surely have known Uncle Tullio. Rapachi was born here; his parents were tenant farmers of my great-grandfather's. He only left to go to the war; afterward, he married Francesca, who bore him seven children, two of whom are still here. Rapachi used to drink barbera and sleep in the barn. I remember him from my childhood, when he showed me how to put up tomatoes and press the grapes. He seemed very old to me even then.

I've never come to the villa without happening to see

him. Sometimes he would call me "sir," sometimes by my first names; he spoke half dialect, half Italian, and had glassy, staring blue eyes. He always greeted me by holding out the two fingers of his right hand; he had been wounded in the war. His sons complained about him, saying he was an old fool who wasted his money getting drunk or running after women. His daughter-in-law and grandchildren would yell at him when they found him asleep at the side of a road or staggering drunkenly around the farmyard.

But, all the same, he was the head of the family; he wore his hat at table, didn't speak, and dipped his bread in the soup. He always went around with a billhook hanging from the string around his waist that held up his trousers, shapeless and baggy. He hardly ever spoke unless addressed. He whistled a lot and chewed tobacco. Though I am in awe of Rapachi, when I realized that he must have known Uncle Tullio well, since he named one of his sons after him, I screwed up my courage and, with the excuse of playing my new role as master, I went to see him. We talked a bit about the farms, he complained about the new chemical fertilizers his sons are using in order to earn more, though they are ruining the land, and we discussed the old genuine products. Then, drinking some barbera, he loosened his tongue, and began by saying to me: "Now, Alberto Claudio, you're the master here. Poor lady, your mother! A saint, she was. And you, sir, are you going to come and live with the rest of us?"

"Who knows? Perhaps I will. You, Rapachi, were born here, weren't you?"

"Yes, sir! And all my sons!"

"You must surely have known my Uncle Tullio."

"Know him? I'll say I did! What a man! He wasn't a master like the others! We used to go hunting together, him and me. Then we both fought on the Carso, and were both in the Fascist squads. Your uncle, by God, he was a brave man! A real man, loyal to his men to the last. What a tragedy, Alberto Claudio, losing a man like that!"

"Rapachi, during the war you didn't by any chance meet a foreign lady, a blonde, a friend of my uncle's?"

"Of course, I met her. She spoke good Italian, with a foreign accent. She was beautiful, something wonderful, all right. And very polite, a real lady. They came here, it must have been 1942 or '43. Your family, they say she was the one who reported your uncle, but that's not possible. They never talked about it because they didn't want anybody to know about that woman; they were always afraid of a scandal. They said she had a lot of German friends, high officers, but you can't make me believe she was a spy. If I can speak freely, I believe she was very attached to the baron."

With this, Rapachi drank another glass and gave me a wink.

"I believe poor Baron Tullio was betrayed by a mountain guide; a question of money. The Fascists would never have touched him; they had too much respect for all he had done. If it hadn't been for that bastard who reported him to the SS, who didn't know who he was, they wouldn't of done a thing to him. There were those dirty laws against you people, but he went right on giving to the party like he had from the beginning. Everybody knew he was the baron Treves and was a Jew and lived in corso Vittorio, but there were orders not to touch him and he knew that. He was a little crazy. He wouldn't have risked his skin, and your aunt's and the kids', without guarantees! No, it was a wartime mix-up. A bastard, you know, a coward who sold them for money. Ah yes, it's unbelievable. I don't mind telling you, Signor Alberto Claudio, your uncle Tullio and me, though I'm an ignorant peasant, we were real friends. But tell me something: why are you so interested in your uncle? In the villa they don't even like to hear his name spoken."

"By chance! Aunt Miriam talked to me about him, then I read his books, I found a diary, some notes, and so I began to get interested in his story, to try to find out the truth about his death. You're the first person to tell me he was betrayed by a guide, that Céleste is innocent. . . . I want to thank you for talking to me about him."

"Listen, Alberto Claudio. Excuse me for calling you by name, but I knew you as a baby, and your mama, too, poor lady. Seeing how interested you are in your uncle Tullio, I think I should confess something to you. Poor man, I'm sure he would be glad for me to tell you. Not long after his death, I happened to find a package, some writings, that I still keep hidden, so nobody can lay a hand on them. Well, I'm old now, the Allies never got their hands on those papers and neither did anybody else. I never told my sons; they don't know a thing. Don't you tell them anything or they'll yell at me, they say I'm always drunk. You, Signor Alberto Claudio, you're educated, like your uncle, and I'll give you that package of papers, I don't know what they are, but you'll be able to figure it out. I'm too ignorant, and I'd have burned them up in the end. In my house they put up with me only because I get two pensions, and money always comes in handy! If it wasn't for my pensions, I'd be in the old folks' home, I would. But I was born here and I want to die in my barn. Yes, sir, I never left this place, except to go to the war. I go into town for the market or to collect the pensions and I go to the cemetery once a year. Your uncle was a gentle-man. And he was very attached to my wife, Francesca, and from our war days he always said to me, 'Rapachi, don't drink so much,' 'Rapachi, you never let go of that bottle!' Poor man, here I am still with my bottle, and he and the baronessa and Francesca are long gone. I don't want to talk too much about my memories. Now I'll go and get those papers for you. You'll have to be patient a bit, because they're buried under a pear tree behind the well in the vineyard."

Rapachi's revelation turned everything upside down again, as he cleared Céleste and introduced the character of the guide who betrayed Uncle Tullio: a hypothesis that immediately seemed plausible to me.

I believe the reading of these new documents will open the way to other truths. I have spoken about this with Thüsis, who is very curious to learn what I find out in those writings.

I told Rapachi that his declarations and the papers he gave me are of supreme importance, in my search for the truth, and now he won't let me out of his sight. He comes to the villa constantly, bringing some grapes, or figs, and he asks me, "How's it going?" or "Is there something else I can do for you?" Coming here and talking to me as an accomplice, knowing that what he gave me is of interest to me, makes him feel important.

It's his revenge on his sons! To be able to speak confidentially of a subject that also interests the master, something that has nothing to do with farming, but is a family secret.

The papers are in a cardboard box, tied with some lengths of twine. They consist of some letters and a copybook, with a black cover. On it is a pasted label with the handwritten word *Notebook*.

17

In this schoolchild's copybook I will write some thoughts
and notes that I don't want others to read. They could be
a series of annotations for a possible book of memoirs,
which I feel it my duty, as a witness, to write when the
war is over. I am unable today to predict the future of my
country and what the Italians will have to face. I fear that
Italy will emerge defeated from the conflict, but I do not
want to accuse the Duce of having dragged us toward the
catastrophe. When he became an ally of the Germans and
considered it proper to declare war on the great democracies, nothing could have led us to believe that the Germans,
under Hitler's mad leadership, would involve us in the
Russian campaign, which inevitably, as it had been for
Napoleon, was the beginning of the disaster. When hos-
tilities started, we fell in behind a victorious Germany that
in the space of a few months had conquered a great part
of Europe and of North Africa. If Mussolini decided to
take an active part in the conflict, it was because he presumed that the fighting would soon end, and with con-
spicuous advantages for our country. The German dicta-
tor's obsessive and immoderate thirst for glory swept us
into other dangerous ventures that the Duce felt called

upon to undertake out of honesty and a sense of honor toward a treaty of alliance that it would have been unworthy to revoke just because things were taking a turn for the worse. We should be proud of the feats of our Alpine troops, who behaved heroically, fighting in extremely adverse conditions with inadequate weapons both on the mountains of Greece and in the Russian plains. The Anglo-American allies seem to control the outcome of the conflict, after a series of sensational victories in North Africa.

At this difficult, sanguinary moment, when the soil of our fatherland is being trampled by enemy troops, I remain unconditionally loyal to the Duce, as I have been constantly since the time when he was a very gifted newspaper editor and, later, when I followed him, as a simple member of an activist squad, in the unforgettable days of the march on Rome. I hope that my compatriots, who in his moments of glory were almost unanimous in their support of the Duce, now, when he faces a difficult situation, will be able to help him to overcome the current crisis and will not turn their backs on him.

The Italians must be convinced that if the war seems to have taken a bad turn, it is actually only a lost battle, and if we follow our leader faithfully, we will find again the path of glory. If German might were to weaken, we could then break with that unnatural ally and find again our Mediterranean destiny. I am sure that in Italy the racial laws would disappear at that time. For that matter, the laws were promulgated for contingent reasons and not out of ideological conviction, for it is well known that the Italians are not a racist people. If the Duce is supported by his compatriots in this difficult period, he will surely recognize and correct those errors of strategic or political evaluation, and will restore to our nation its proud, Italian self-sufficiency, that healthy and strong character that he was able to make evident before the war.

This notebook is for no one but me; I have decided to make notes in order to remember, to arrest sensations, images, private things and historic things, without asking myself what I'll do with them. I write as I feel, with no link between one thought and the next. I want to speak with myself. I seem to find myself in a double, quadruple position. . . . First of all, I want to admit in writing that during these dark and tattered years, in which I have lived as an outcast, passive, rejected by history, I have rid myself of some basic uncertainties. Even though I was aware that it is contrary to the behavior of a true Fascist, I have given free rein to my homosexuality, too long repressed. No longer able to dissimulate that need that had lived within me since puberty like a germ or a parasite, unable to work it off in war adventures, rallies, punitive Fascist actions, I have sought out boys. Poor boys, generally young, dark, strong; and though I have remained fond of Allegra, I have spent whole days in cheap furnished rooms, releasing an eroticism castrated for too long. Those secret days have given me the moral strength to bear the humiliation of being different, separated from my companions and, still worse, seeing my ideas becoming more and more anti-historical and the party I believed in becoming more and more corrupt and weak.

But the greatest paradox I have experienced recently is that, while I go on seeing boys sporadically, I have fallen passionately, overwhelmingly in love with a foreign woman, blond and unattainable. C. is the official fiancée of a well-known Fascist authority, a man I like and respect.

I believe my passion for C. can be attributed to her double personality; on the one hand she is very sweet, with occasionally childish attitudes; and on the other, she has a sensuality and a way of creating erotic situations that is really dangerous. I believe she has fallen in love with me. She is attracted by my ugliness, my mediocrity, the fact that I'm a Jew. For her I am forbidden fruit, inconceivable as a lover, in the eyes of the world.

C. is a convinced Fascist, but her Fascism originally derived from the fact that in the charismatic figure of Mussolini and hence in the Mussolinian prototype of the perfect, conquering male, Italian and Fascist, C. has virtually found her perfect aesthetic ideal.

Now her relationship with me, thanks to a coincidence of circumstances, represents that extra something necessary to complete her satisfaction. She has experienced the most glorious moment of the Fascist era, as the devoted mistress of a young and promising official, who personified every ideal of Latin beauty, but now, though she is still with him, she enjoys betraying him with a man whose sensitivity is closer to her own, who is also a devoted Fascist, but ugly and Jewish.

I have employed a number of words to say that the Fascist official, perfect symbol of statuesque Latin beauty, appeals to us, we like and envy him; but he isn't enough for us. Our affinities are not revealed and rationalized, but both of us feel the certitude that we have finally found ourselves. I believe there is something else we have in common. Though we are both naturally attracted by solar, victorious characters, like the Duce, in both of us there is a melancholy side, unconfessed, that impels us toward an attitude of renunciation.

We have both chosen the nationalist provincialism of Mussolini's Italy, against a kind of life that, by birth or by education, we would otherwise be destined to lead: a brilliant, cosmopolitan life. She could easily be living in New York, Paris, Switzerland, as a lady of the great international world; and I could be a typical rich and refined Jew, living only to satisfy his tastes as an aesthete and a collector. We could be free, even in these war years, within the aesthetic confines of a certain luxury, closely involved with culture, enjoying travel, leisure. On the contrary, we have chosen to live in a country that, for different reasons, doesn't really accept us, but where, in fact, our aestheticism, melancholy, renunciation find their satisfaction. For us it is a bet against history. I know that what I have written is poorly expressed and confused, but I wanted to tell how I happened to find, in a person who is my antithesis, far from my world, the woman who might be called my soul mate. In my affair with C. I find also the satisfaction of certain Nietzschean and Wagnerian tendencies of mine.

Today I want to write about Turin. About how unusual living in Turin is in this period. For me everything has changed. I am no longer Baron Treves, but Cavalier Luigi Podda. One of my sons has died of an incurable disease; the other two boys are abroad. Allegra has detached herself from me and has taken refuge in the mountains with our daughter, while I live in a rented apartment in corso Vittorio (I have already written this in my diary). I feel as if I had become the protagonist of a Pirandello play. I live in my city, where the population has changed; my friends and acquaintances have emigrated or in any case left, the few Fascist companions still living here have invented for me the false identity of Luigi Podda, and though they are aware that I am in Turin, in order to protect me they pretend not to know me. So I live between two women: Esther Moscati, a Jewish girl who takes care of the house and my everyday needs, and C., the person I am in love with, who appears and disappears. There are also numerous moments of solitude, in which I write, read, listen to music, play the piano. My Fascist companions need my money; and their protection, I must admit, has allowed me to buy myself a false position as the threatened victim of racism, when, like everyone else, I really am threatened, constantly, by the menaces of a city at war. Every night there are air raids. But this disorder, this sense of precariousness, the food shortages, the uncomfortable transportation make my condition as racial outlaw less important. For the present I don't want to complain. There are times when I seem to be young again, as in my army days. To procure the money I need for survival, with the help of a middleman, I have sold two apartment buildings to a black-market profiteer; and I have hidden the money in various places, which I hope are sufficiently safe. Mussolini's fall seems to me an unutterable tragedy for the country; my hopes for national solidarity have gone up in smoke. As always, I am too romantic! They kicked Mussolini out overnight; the king and Badoglio are in command of the country, and it would seem that in Italy there were never any Fascists (I'm talking about the majority of Italians). It grieves me to think that Mussolini was betrayed by his own high officials. Those men who owed him everything were capable only of turning their back on him at the moment of difficulty.

I could easily exploit this dirty situation, go and report to Badoglio as a retired officer; but if I were to do that, I could never face myself in the mirror again out of shame. I wonder, on the contrary, with uneasiness what will become of us true Fascists. I can't believe that they have all switched allegiance overnight. But what will be left of Fascism without the guidance of the Duce? Nobody ever thought of the succession. It's incredible, the way we deceive ourselves, thinking that certain people can be immortal and unmovable.

Unfortunately it's necessary to wait and the only thing to do is to live day by day through these changes. The eighth of September was a disgrace and a disaster better passed over in silence. Badoglio sold Italy to the Allies. The northern part of the peninsula has become a German colony, and it would be hard to describe the disorder that reigns in the cities. Turin is teeming with deserters — those who don't want to fight alongside the Germans, and who refuse to join Badoglio.

Fortunately the Duce has been freed by the Germans and has returned to the political scene. Under his leadership the Italian Social Republic has been proclaimed. In his photographs the Duce seems aged, and in his eyes I can read gloomy thoughts and dire presentiments. Though the new republic splits Italy into two factions, practically speaking, it will restore a certain order to that part of the country occupied by the Germans. The figure of the Duce, the republic of Salò, the Fascist militia represent in any case for us Italians an attempt not to feel completely subjugated by the Germans. Luckily Allegra has taken refuge in a safe place, and C. is with me again. Despite everything that is happening around us, she is more and more demanding; she would want me to drown all worries in an overwhelming passion, as far as possible from real or tangible things. At times we talk about afterward. We don't know what "afterward" means, but, like all lovers, we need to think of an imaginary future for ourselves. We ask ourselves, pretending not to be certain, what we would do if the Germans were to lose the war, or else we torture ourselves, asking what would happen if they were to win. How hard it is to remain loyal Fascists, not really knowing anymore which side we're on, because all sides have become equally odious.

I am a retired officer who swore fidelity to the king, and at the time of the march on Rome, I went to great pains to convince some of my more extremist companions that Mussolini was acting for the good of the nation when he renounced his republican ideas, sacrificing them to the idea of the monarchy. Now it is the monarchy that first turned its back on Fascism and brought about Mussolini's downfall. Fascism has risen again as a republic, under the aegis of the Germans. Our country has become such a historical mess that nobody knows where he is anymore, or on whose side. For the first time since the racial laws were decreed, I actually feel in danger because I'm Jewish. I don't believe that the few friends I still have among the leading figures in the Social Republic are powerful enough to save me from the Gestapo, if it were necessary. The thing I fear is that, since my identity as Luigi Podda was given me by my Fascist companions, it would be very easy, in times like these, for someone to report me anonymously. True, the Italian people are not racist and, still less, anti-Semitic, but even so, as in any other nation, and especially in a confused and precarious historical moment, there are certain people who wouldn't think twice about trading the life of a Jew for a bit of money or a scrap of cheese. So for the first time I feel threatened, unsafe, and I am afraid. At times, I must confess, I am even afraid of C. I have always been anti-German, whereas she is pro-German, especially nowadays, when things are going badly for Germany. This attitude is part of her masochism, and in addition, every time we have a quarrel, she finds it exciting, more erotic, to make threats. She convinces me that our love must never, at any cost, grow weaker, because if I showed any sign of wearying, she would be quite capable of reporting me. I know she says this because she enjoys playing a dangerous game, and it seems to her that this new element gives our love a sense of risk and makes it more romantic and theatrical. Loving a woman who could become an enemy involves a tension that, though I understand it, surely is no help to my nervous system. Knowing that at any hour of the day or night I could be arrested by an anonymous gentleman from the Gestapo terrifies me. It's one thing to play, to defy fate by saying: "I won't take shelter, and let the bomb fall where it pleases." This is a risk that anyone who chooses to run it must experience. But it's quite another matter to know that your own survival depends on a wink, a murmured word from someone else. I suppose that for some people this must be almost a pleasure, a kind of revenge for the uncertainty of our lives, being able to vent your ferocity on an unwelcome individual, having him eliminated by others, who will soil their hands in your place. What an extraordinary opportunity: to commit a murder without being punished!

I suffer because of the separation from my family. We have lived apart for too many months, with sporadic news, often secondhand. It would be great if we could all meet for New Year's. I don't know what to do, because I don't want to leave C. during the holidays, still I would like to see Allegra and the children. But the thought of separating in this period is always painful, full of anguish, as if it contained the seed of betrayal, a definitive flavor. But then: after the war? What would happen between me and C. if the war really did end and we both came out of it alive? What would happen to me and C.? Perhaps I should decide to leave everything behind and go and live abroad with her, say in Argentina. But this doesn't go with my new temperament.

I don't even dare think of after the war, of Italy transformed into an Anglo-American colony. I would never be able to adapt, certainly. For almost five years I have been leading a marginal life. For how many more years must I accept this fate? What does it mean, to live always as an outcast, because you are against the course of history? Perhaps it would be better if I went straight to the Gestapo and turned myself in, and put an end to it. At least they would eliminate me and I wouldn't have to face further humiliations. It horrifies me to think that if I survive I will have to watch a civil war passively, as someone not wanted by either side.

I have even dreamed of going to see the Duce in Salò. Of going to confess to him, explaining my difficult present situation, asking his advice. I am almost certain he would advise me to escape to safety with my family.

I don't have the courage to leave C. I know that if I tell her it's only for a few days, she might avenge herself, because she would think I was only making an excuse in order to abandon her.

I should be ashamed of myself for writing certain things; I feel so base; but I am suffering, and my nervous system can barely tolerate this unhealthy, precarious situation. And besides, I love C., but I feel she is my enemy, and this frightens me.

I drag along in this mood, here in Turin, where for the first time I feel a prisoner and an alien. At night I don't leave the house, and I imagine the desolation of the empty streets, where only a few German soldiers move about, knowing their days are numbered. For them, who triumphantly occupied Paris, it must seem scant consolation, occupying, and with difficulty, our little Turin.

I don't want to make myself ridiculous, expressing pity for the fate of the German soldiers; but I don't envy them their destiny. For them, who really did dominate Europe, this grievous and humiliating defeat must be a horrible tragedy. I don't dare think of the dejecting sight that Germany will offer after the war.

I have heard from Rapachi, our peasant and my faithful Fascist companion, that the villa has been occupied by the Nazis and turned into a convalescent hospital for officers.

I often think how sad a true love story can be. There are moments when the two feel united and inseparable, and then a trifle suffices to sweep it all away. In passionate love there is a possessive and childish aspect that can be the antithesis of friendship. Now, while on the one hand C. and I spend beautiful, mad moments together, irrational and unforgettable moments, when our subconscious lets itself be overwhelmed, at other times the friction of our character differences gets the upper hand, our intolerance of the precariousness of this period and, at the same time, a terror that our love will finish because it is fed by this same precariousness.

If at certain times C. seems a woman without reactions, limp, passive, superficial, desiring only lovemaking and erotic play, at other times I realize that this passiveness is a defense. My life is all taken up with my family problems, my problems as a Jew and as a Fascist, and I wonder how to lead my life in these murky waters and I don't think often enough that she also has her life and she's in a dangerous position chiefly because she loves me. A woman like C. would have countless ways of saving herself, finding refuge, preparing a less uncertain postwar. Instead, she remains here in Turin, leads a double life between me and her Fascist, and knows very well that both stories can only end badly. It's all very well for me to believe that she enjoys letting herself drift, carried by the stream, to the end: but I'm certain she suffers. She suffers at the vain life we are forced to live. I know I could still find a way of escaping with her and getting out of this desolation, but I lack the strength, the conviction. I wouldn't know where to begin to find the severity necessary to making a choice: events seem more powerful than I am. This is why C. and I plunge into the whirlpool of the senses, to escape all dialogue, all planning, all truth. Historical events will manage our life. It is very sad to be a doomed man, who absolutely cannot know any longer where he is, because the world in which he lives no longer corresponds to him.

Too absorbed in my thoughts, these last few months I have moved away from the reality of the city and the things that surround me. This morning, on the contrary, on waking up I noticed that the streets are covered by a fine snowy blanket, and snow is still falling: a thick, dense fall, with big flakes that remain on the ground. I imagined how beautiful the hills must be, cloaked in white, and I felt a desire to go and see. Snow sweetens and tempers memories and sensations, and today I felt I was enjoying a moment of truce. For a long time I haven't felt any real desires and my life has been a constant succession of anguish and terror. Watching those slow, clean flakes fall, I wanted to go out, to breathe that cold and purified air. Bombings, war, Nazi-Fascists or Allies, the snow was always the same, white and cottony. And so, ignoring the danger of being recognized on the street, I put on a big dark overcoat, cut in military style, fur-lined, and I set off along the arcades of corso Vittorio. The city was beautiful and cleansed, and when I reached Platti's, I stopped and drank an aperitif. Through the window I saw that in corso Re Umberto there was a group of children having a snowball fight, as I had seen my children behave, and as I had done with my brothers. . . . Coming out of Platti's I decided to head for La

Crocetta, and when I turned into corso Duca di Genova, I felt a shudder. Near there, at the beginning of the war, I used to go in the early afternoon to visit a boy. Who knows where he is now?

Returning, I wanted to take a look at the Valentino park and the embankment under the snow. In my brisk pace, as I occasionally broke the silence with a whispered snatch of song, I could sense vibrations that seemed to be what I imagine is the joy of living. In that cold and virile walk, I felt my manly blood, my soldier's blood, flowing in a different way, and for once my thoughts were not torments. Now I am home again, tired, chilled, and happy at having rediscovered my love of nature, which is more beautiful and stronger than anything else.

This is where Tullio's notebook stops. Unfortunately I have learned nothing about his end, not a clue. Though I have grasped other aspects of his personality, I have perhaps done nothing but muddle my ideas even more.

Stuck in the last pages of the notebook there are the drafts of two letters, which give me still some hope of discovering a secret: they are dated December 1943.

Dear Ada Louise,

I am writing you this letter, but I still don't know if I will have the courage to send it to you. It's a confession, and I want your advice. We seem to have an unspoken agreement, to spend this grim period in an atmosphere of heedlessness. An exacerbated heedlessness that conceals fear, a fear of having to separate in order to find normality again, go back to our families, and live in a new world to which we will have to become accustomed.

The two of us, recently, have talked often of death. You threaten me, saying you will turn me in if I go off even for a single day. The future seems to me contrary to every aspiration of mine. I really don't know why I should have to bear coexistence with the neo-enthusiasts of a neo-freedom. Perhaps if you were to report me, you would be giving me a real present. I would be sent away and then shot. It may seem egoistic for me to ask your help in eluding this world, but whether I am dead or alive, you will have to live elsewhere, without me. It's sad to realize one is too weak, too lacking in courage to fight to keep a great love alive. I know it would be beautiful to be able to spend Christmas together, in corso Vittorio, but I feel it's my duty to join Allegra in the mountains. I haven't seen her for too long, I know she's not well, and in addition I've been told she has organized an absurd and dangerous plan: to bring back our sons from Switzerland for a few days, so that all of us can be together again. I don't know why I've written you this letter, which I don't have the courage to give you and lack the strength to destroy.

Tullio

My beloved,

Why are we the victims of a horrible fate that forces us to live apart? Why are we resigned to thinking that our love can't have any future?

How I wish that the fabric of talk and erotic games that unites us at night could last forever!

It's horrible to be living in the twilight of an era, which drains the enthusiasm from a great love. Perhaps I'm the one who's too complicated, and as I keep seeing myself sinking into a grim and squalid future, I waste the scant energy left me, unable to overcome my dull listlessness, and decide to carry you off. I can no longer respect myself, and sometimes I even enjoy this sense of abandonment to destiny. I can't get used to the fact that my children will have to grow up in a world different from the one I would have wanted for them. In any case, they are still young and will be able to find themselves a place. But what about us?

A tender embrace.

Tullio

These letters are only the expression of a sense of desolation and melancholy in Tullio. Now all I can do is wait for Thüsis's return, which should be imminent. I'm curious to hear her impressions of the notebook.

There are places where the handwriting is so different from the diary's that I can't help wondering if it was actually Tullio who wrote it . . .

18

Thüsis hadn't telephoned me for three days and I couldn't figure out what had happened. Three days of silence when you're in love seem a lifetime, and it's incredible how many negative explanations can occur to you in a short while. Out of desperation more than anything else, to be able somehow to talk about her, I called the Pensione Europa, where they told me she had just gone out. I had a feeling that my negative thoughts hadn't been completely unjustified. It was strange that she had come back and had gone immediately to class without giving me any sign of life. I knew it would be best for me to wait in the house for her to call me, but as I was thinking this, I was already on my way to the dance school.

I saw her at once: she was wearing black tights, working at the barre. I watched her in silence as Tanya spoke to her in a stern tone, giving her orders I couldn't understand, while she meekly obeyed and changed position, looking at herself in a great mirror. The teacher wore some heavy gray ankle warmers, and waved a long cane as she gave instructions. In one corner of the room a man was playing the piano. Thüsis was so intent that I let her finish the lesson and went to her only when it was over. I was afraid she would receive me with aggression; but on the contrary, when she saw me she smiled and flung herself into my arms, clinging tightly to me. I heard her murmur, "Thanks for coming." Then, in a loud voice, she said: "Wait for me. I'll change in a moment and be right with you. I have so many things to tell you!"

We sat at Mulassano's in piazza Castello, where we ordered some sandwiches and two glasses of white wine. Thüsis smoked constantly and seemed in excellent humor. Instead of enjoying the moment of sweetness and waiting for her to tell me everything, I immediately asked her: "Where have you been? Why did you disappear? Why didn't you phone me? Did you forget about me? How long have you been back?"

"What is this, the third degree? I can see how you respect me! I got back late last night, exhausted by an endless train trip, and when I woke up this morning I decided to go to Tanya to find out the horrible condition I'm in. I had to accept the unexpected hospitality of an elderly gentleman from whose house I couldn't telephone. All I can say is that from Leghorn I've brought you another anecdote, to add to all the others of our research, and it contradicts the hypothesis of your farmer who takes it for granted that Uncle Tullio was betrayed by a guide and killed by the SS."

"What does all this have to do with the fact that you didn't telephone?"

"While I was still on Corsica, a person gave me the name of the shipowner in Leghorn who arranged for Aunt Céleste to escape at night on a sailboat, as far as Bastia. This gentleman was quite willing to see me and he told me that, in fact, as a favor to a friend, he had helped Céleste board a boat for Bastia and the man with her one for Nice. I asked him if he remembered Aunt Céleste's escort. From the description I realized it was Uncle Tullio. So our Baron Treves sailed in 1944 for Nice and from there he meant to go on to South America, at the war's end."

"But the Germans killed him in 1943 with Aunt Allegra and the children! How can he have escaped to France in '44?"

"It seems absurd, but it's plausible; and he could still be alive. Nobody can identify the dead once they're reduced to ashes. So it could have gone like this: during that Christmas–New Year's holiday of 1943–1944, Céleste managed to prevent Tullio from going to the mountains to see his family. Meanwhile, a guide who had led the boys through the mountains to spend the holidays with their parents, having realized there was something mysterious about it and that these were rich people, turned them in. The Germans raided the refuge where Allegra was living and killed them all. Since the boys had told the guide they were going to visit their parents, it was taken for granted that Tullio was also present, and the newspapers were informed that 'Baron Treves and his family died in an accident in the mountains.' Other newspapers wrote that they had been killed by a band of subversives. Tullio, seeing the news, could hardly go to German headquarters and contradict it. So, with the identity of Luigi Podda or under some other name, he hid here and there with Céleste, until they finally managed to escape from Leghorn."

"But look, if that was so, why didn't they go to Corsica together?"

"Because they were both suspect and the settling of scores then was bloodthirsty, so it was better for each to hide on his own. I can't say, at this point, how and when they met again afterward. I don't know if Tullio is still alive."

"To be sure, if that hypothesis is true, it would upset all our investigations. We have to go and talk with Céleste, because she's the only one who knows if Uncle Tullio escaped or not, and if that man the Leghorn shipowner mentioned was Tullio or not."

"Unfortunately the shipowner I spoke with doesn't remember the name; he can only say that the man had sparse blond hair, pale eyes, was short and a bit stout. That's all I know. Furthermore, I doubt that Aunt Céleste, who after 1944 made up the role of widow of Fascism for herself, will now reveal that she and Tullio Treves have lived for forty years in the shadows. I also doubt that, after years of exile, he in Argentina and she on Corsica, they then met again in Paris and moved to New York. Tullio would have surfaced somehow!"

"Not necessarily, and this could be yet another fantasy of theirs. Besides, she could have helped him escape and then not have seen him again because of some mysterious series of circumstances. You're right: it's a hypothesis that erases everything else. To sum up: the two of them would still be alive, and Aunt Allegra and the children were killed because they were betrayed by an informer. This way the idea of anyone else being guilty is eliminated. In that case, perhaps your aunt will confess without any problems. After all, she simply helped to save a poor Jew who had lost his whole family."

"Yes, you could be right, but it sounds too simple to me, and something tells me that this isn't all that simple."

"I have some things to do here, but at the beginning of October we could go and visit your aunt."

"I can't come."

"What do you mean?"

"No. It's too expensive, and I would embarrass her. I don't want to see my mother or Uncle Bill, and besides I have to finish with the school."

"Listen, don't worry about the fare; we don't have to

call up your uncle, and you can easily take a week off from school."

Thüsis lit a cigarette and studied me severely. I sensed that I had said things I shouldn't say. "Alberto Claudio, you've seen my house on Corsica, haven't you?"

"Yes, but what's that got to do with it?"

"You saw how Spartan it is. Well, that's how I've decided to lead my life. Till now I've never seen anything through to its conclusion. I've always been sidetracked by laziness, inconstancy, whims. You mustn't believe I don't want to discover the truth of this story; but I want to take my school seriously, I don't have the money for the trip, and I don't want you to pay my way. I know I may sound foolishly proud to you, but this is how Daffy brought me up. I want to live with you, I told you I've fallen in love with you, I love you, but I don't want to be kept just because you're rich now and everything's easy . . ."

"But what's that got to do with it? We're going to New York to meet Céleste! Then you'll come back, finish your school, and I'll write a book or go back to work for a newspaper."

"No, you're going to New York alone and you'll talk with Céleste. You'll tell her you came across her while you were studying the life of your uncle. But I mustn't be there; otherwise she won't talk."

"But look, she's your aunt, you're the one who discovered this whole story! It seems right for you to meet her."

"I'll meet her when I've finished here. It scares me a little, the thought of meeting her now."

PART SEVEN

Céleste

19

I spent a difficult, tedious month in Turin, dealing with
my affairs, unable to convince Thüsis to go with me to
New York. In order to meet Céleste I had to get in touch
with Uncle Bill, who was presumably back in the city,
and Thüsis didn't want to see him.

I became persuaded that there was no point insisting and
that I had to go alone. As an outsider, I would have a better
chance of getting information out of Céleste. Also I believe
Thüsis wanted me to take charge of the whole thing, so
that she could devote herself completely to the dance.

In any case, that tug-of-war, "oh come on, why won't
you come, please come," was growing tiresome. So, with
reluctance, I flew alone to New York, where Bill and Nancy
were waiting for me.

Bill welcomed me jovially, as he had at Ajaccio, and
immediately insisted I have supper with them. I told him
I was in America to continue my studies and I'd be grateful
if he would arrange for me to meet his aunt Céleste, as he
had promised on Corsica. I realized that the idea upset
him, but being such a man of the world, he couldn't refuse,
and he promised to do everything in his power, though

he wasn't sure of succeeding, given her unpredictability.

Bill and Nancy seemed very happy to manage the New York stay of a young European intellectual, engaged to their adored niece.

Thüsis had explained her absence with a sweet letter, saying how important it was for her to continue her studies in Turin, and in closing, she entrusted me to their care.

I spent a week socializing, with artists, stylists, actresses, and millionaires, in the most elegant homes and restaurants in New York. For the weekend Bill and Nancy took me to Connecticut, to the house of a photographer friend, and everyone was extremely cordial. So I lived amid bubbles of champagne and gobs of whipped cream, a succession of parties and dinners, trivial chats alternating with an incredible eagerness to discuss politics, art, money, and journeys; and gossip. I let myself be led among strangers who spoke to me and then were immediately bored the moment they learned I was in America only briefly, and therefore wasn't interesting. The most frequent question was: "When are you going back to Europe?" after I had answered no to the question "Have you come to New York to live?" I understood why Thüsis didn't want to come here, to be smothered in hugs, in this world that was always made to seem very easygoing, though it was basically hard and pitiless.

Observing Nancy and Bill closely, I wondered what kept them together. Perhaps their socializing habits, the pleasure of talking, of going to the right places, of being present everywhere. Bill's painting was a pretext, and he worked at it like a white-collar employee between social engagements. He turned out a lot of paintings, all alike, and sold them at an annual show in a Madison Avenue gallery, preceded or followed by a party given in his honor, where all the celebrities of New York were to be seen.

I didn't dare insist on the meeting with Céleste, because from time to time, about once every two days, Bill would give me a wink and say, "I'm working on it for you. We'll hope for the best. She's an eccentric woman, you know." As nothing happened, I called Thüsis in Turin, to tell her of my dismay at wasting all this time. She urged me to be patient, and hung up quickly, saying I was spending too much money.

As I waited to meet Céleste, I visited a number of museums, went to the opera, and called on an elderly writer who had been a friend of my mother's. He is a strange character, who writes in several languages and lives in poverty because he has spent most of his life quarreling with his publishers, with his editors, or employers. The moment he discovered someone had taken the liberty of eliminating a semicolon in a text of his, he would withdraw the manuscript. He has been living in New York since before the war, in voluntary political exile. Physically, he looks like a nineteenth-century gentleman, and various personalities overlap in him: the dandy, the curmudgeon, the American intellectual, the Tolstoyan idealist, and the passionate reader of Homer, Dante, Plato, whom he reads and rereads constantly. He keeps eccentric hours; he sleeps from four in the afternoon till eleven at night, then he gets up, writes until four in the morning and then, dressing like a bum, he walks around the streets of New York, long walks that last until midmorning. Then he goes home, bathes, changes, and fixes his lunch. His house consists of two communicating rooms, fairly dusty, where you can see nothing but papers, notes, books, typewriters, and suitcases. If you are invited to lunch, you are given a ritual dish of lentils, which you eat with the plate carefully balanced on a pile of papers. I told him about my mother's death. He was silent, as if seized by a fit of metaphysical absence. "Too bad! Great woman!"

We talked about my grandfather Dimitri and their occasional meetings in Paris. "One of the few surviving people with whom I can still speak Russian."

Finally I asked him if he knew Céleste.

"Unfortunately, I do know her. She's a shit, a liar, and a Fascist. One of those shits who express contempt for money, say that the rich are vulgar, that we should all live simply, but naturally she only goes around with people who are loaded, and she wouldn't come across with me because I don't have a cent."

Finally Bill called me at eight a.m. to inform me that his aunt would see me in the early afternoon. He would come and pick me up, take me there, and stay long enough to introduce me.

Céleste lives in a co-op on Central Park West. The door was opened by a shy black maid in a kind of nurse's uniform. She led us into a spacious living room, full of light. An elegant lady, her ash-blond hair dressed very carefully, was seated in an armchair; she was wearing black. She looked at me with her big blue eyes, shortsighted, distant, as she dissimulated her interest in me; and, in a trilling voice, she immediately said, "I'm so sorry Bill didn't tell me sooner of your visit. I'm afraid I don't have an extra ticket for Béjart. And it's too late to do anything about it now; they're absolutely sold out."

"Thank you so much for the kind thought, but it doesn't matter that much. Fortunately, I saw the company last autumn, in Paris."

"Ah, but this is different. Tonight there's the premiere of a new ballet, specially choreographed for this American tour."

Bill, in the meantime, had served himself a port. Now he joined in the conversation, imposing a light, witty tone. Nephew and aunt talked about various art shows and concerts in the city. In their mannered way of moving and speaking I seemed to recognize a family code, a necessity to feel chic, intelligent, critical, and most of all, beautiful and superior to everyone else; and, with this, a frank contempt of everything that might bear the faintest resemblance to the banal or the déjà vu.

Before our chat could become too intense and lead us away from the real purpose of my visit, Bill obligingly said: "I must run. I'll leave you two to your tête-à-tête."

I realized that I had remained silent to observe the good-mannered exchange between aunt and nephew; though we were in modern America, it suggested those half-French, half-Russian dialogues in the plays of Chekhov.

They hated each other. Bill couldn't stand his aunt's ambiguous behavior and could never forget her for having always favored his brother, Daffy. Céleste found Bill colorless, and couldn't forgive him for not having died in Daffy's place. And further, she was annoyed that the social world had opened its arms wide for Bill, the man of culture, and had turned its back on his brother, who was antisocial.

From the moment I saw Céleste, I noticed that Thüsis resembled her very much, though the niece was much more beautiful and straightforward. Céleste, on the other hand, was constantly acting, like a performer onstage.

I was left alone with the legendary Céleste, in her large sunny living room, furnished with strange Palermo-baroque armchairs, in the shape of shells, and a baby grand piano.

To lure her into speaking about what concerned me, I told her that I was interested in Egyptology and that I had recently discovered, to my great delight, that the Egyptian

Museum in Turin was the third most important in the world, after Cairo and London. She promptly interrupted me and, as I had hoped, she said: "Ah, Turin! I know Turin well, I lived there from time to time during the last war. It's such an elegant city, surrounded by those magnificent hills."

"I don't want to seem indiscreet, but I was almost certain you knew Turin. You see, it's a strange coincidence, and I think it deserves an explanation. As I told you, my work in Egyptology took me to Turin, where I have some relatives, who have put me up on various occasions during these past years. By chance, in their library, I found some books by a sort of distant uncle of mine, Tullio Treves, and also some letters and diaries in which you are often mentioned, especially in 1942 and '43, first simply as C., then as Céleste, then as Ada Louise. I found out that this person might be you, madame, through a friend of mine, after I'd given her the diary to read: Thüsis Foulk, the daughter of your nephew Daffy. I hope you don't mind my taking the liberty to come and see you and to speak frankly with you."

"Mind? Why should I mind? It's an extraordinary coincidence, isn't it? You don't look a thing like him. You are so tall and dark! Who would ever have said it? Yes, it's true, during that period I was quite close to poor Tullio; but it's a sad story, and all these years have gone by. It's painful for me to talk about it. Still, I'm glad you've told me you are poor Tullio's nephew, and I must confess I find it very moving."

"As a matter of fact, I've heard so many conflicting stories about my uncle and his tragic end that I've developed a real interest in it all; and I'd like to discover the truth, if I can. His memory is clouded by so much slander, so many insinuations. In his writings he seems a man tormented by passions that are in conflict with the stiff, bourgeois education he had been given. I quite understand that you wouldn't want to talk about those sad, bitter days of the past; but you may be the only person who could help me find out who that man really was and what were the real circumstances of his death. And there's another thing: an old farmhand, who knew him well, actually told me a rumor that Tullio hadn't been killed at all, that he had escaped to South America."

"My dear young friend, it has been very kind of you to come and see me. But what do the memories of a woman in love matter? These are personal secrets, and obviously I can't discuss them. And besides, love blurs and blunts, enlarges, diminishes; so any opinion of mine would be partial. If you want to discover the man your uncle was and, as I seem to understand, clear his name, all I can tell you is that he was a person of extreme sensitivity; oh yes, irresponsible, but only in certain fleeting moments of euphoria. His real aim in life was to understand what was truly just, proper, for a man. He believed that for every human being there is a truth, and our life should be the constant search for that truth. He was best-known as a former officer, a Fascist, a man of business, but he was at heart a philosopher, always seeking a meaning in human life. In the autumn of 1943 we saw each other often, and as he saw the horrors of war destroying his country, and the even more horrible civil war, he kept asking himself, in anguish and despair, what his behavior as an individual should be, as history was bearing down on us. The triumph of the Anglo-Americans and the Soviets was imminent by then; and for him it was a very grave, personal tragedy. He didn't want to survive in a country that had become a Soviet or an American colony. He felt humiliated by his passiveness, his impotence in the face of events. It made him suffer to see Mussolini, who had always been his guide and master, transformed into a puppet in the Germans' hands. And, mind you, Tullio was a Jew and had to live cautiously, under an assumed name. He often asked himself why he should go on living, when he continued to believe in something that no longer existed. Every day his beliefs became more abstract, unreal; and things he had been loyal to for years crumbled away before his eyes."

"From what you're telling me, it sounds as if he was very close to suicide."

"I'd prefer not to commit myself. Yes, he talked about death, but as I told you, his talk became increasingly vague and confused. It was as if he had already walked out of life. With me he preferred not to talk about his feelings; he would joke and chat about trivial matters, turning his back on the world and the bombs."

"But didn't he express any desire to leave Italy, to start a new life?"

"He had no desire for a new life and didn't want to leave. He preferred living with me in unreality."

"Do you know if he was killed? I can't believe the official story, of Tullio going to see his family in the mountains and being slaughtered with them. I'm almost certain he came to a different end. I have a feeling he survived."

"You have a lively imagination. I realize that the idea of his surviving, his having a separate destiny, can be fascinating; but I'm afraid he came to a much less romantic end. I don't know if he was killed alone or with his family. It was during the New Year's holiday and I was elsewhere, with another person. He had talked to me about a visit to Allegra, but hadn't said anything specific, and then, from the papers, I learned the news of his death. Since then I have considered myself in mourning. Since his death I have been alone forever. I really couldn't tell you if he was reported or if he turned himself in, to make an end of it; if he was with his family, if it was the Nazis who killed him or the partisans. Since I was very devoted to him, I have always refused to believe he reported himself voluntarily, as many people insist. It may be feminine pride, but I believe he loved me too much to decide to leave me alone. Furthermore, though he was depressed by the adverse circumstances, he had always remained a soldier, and so he wouldn't have committed suicide. And also I believe that, though he complained that he had no place in history, he was really very much attached to life or, in particular, to the ritual of living. In any case I'm talking too much, because I don't know anything, and perhaps I should have made some effort to know more, and in those days I would have been in a position to use the power of certain acquaintances of mine to have justice done, if the murderers had been discovered. But at that point Tullio was dead and no vendetta would bring him back to life. So I decided to wear mourning and avoid finding out the truth. I know that some people have talked of my being an informer, but that's all gossip. What importance can the motives of the end have?"

"For me it's a personal matter. I'd only like to know how my uncle died — also because, as I told you before, I suspect he survived."

"I hate to disillusion you. I'm sorry I can't say you're right, that I have kept Tullio hidden in the cellar all these years and, if you like, I'd go and call him for you. If he were alive, he'd have gone to live in Paris, which was his favorite city. As you see, I can't help you in any way to unravel your tangle of suspicions, but I seem to sense in you a special sweetness that reminds me of Tullio, and so I've allowed myself to be carried away . . ."

"Oh, what you tell me about my uncle is extremely

interesting. I would never have believed you hid him or anything like that; but perhaps you might have had some notion or have found out that he had survived, and then you might have lost track of him."

"His family chose to turn him into a 'Jewish martyr,' for fear that he might be remembered as a 'fierce anti-Semitic Fascist.' Tullio had decided that the best way to lead his life was to embrace a cause and to stick with it to the end. He would never have embraced another out of opportunism, because that would have been cowardly. For years he had played a role with talent and enthusiasm, but even the most committed actor, when the play is over, leaves his dressing room and becomes a man, so he during those last months had become a man without a part; and he didn't want to play any other."

"It's interesting, this way you see Uncle Tullio in the last years."

"You mustn't be ashamed of this relative of yours, dear boy. Cherish his writings, and if you come to see me again, I'll let you read some beautiful letters I've saved, which I often reread, because they give me strength to go on living. Now you must forgive me, but I am an old woman, and this unexpected emotion has tired me. But don't forget: come and see me again before you leave!"

I emerged from that encounter hypnotized by Céleste's spell, reassured and convinced by her words. So I could be proud of my Uncle Tullio; it was irrelevant, to learn whose hand had killed him; and it was naturally out of the question that this lady could have had even the remotest connection with his mysterious death.

As soon as I got back to the hotel, I called Thüsis to talk about Céleste. She kept saying: "All right, all right! You can tell me in person when you come back."

A moment later Bill called me, to ask my impression of his aunt.

"Extraordinary!"

"So you let yourself be seduced, as could have been foreseen. Now you'll tell me you also found her cultivated and intelligent."

"Yes, she has a strange way of speaking. I was struck by the feline look in her eyes, and the way she moves her hands. Those gnarled, dry hands, so carefully tended."

"I hope you never see another side of Céleste. Her perversity, like a poisonous snake."

"Why, I found her sweet and intelligent."

"I hope you never run into her when she's drunk. But if it was helpful for your research . . ."

"It was. And thanks for having introduced me to her; she is really an important source."

Since Céleste asked me to go and see her again, I let a few days pass, then I telephoned.

Politely, she said: "Come tomorrow after lunch."

I turned up as instructed, in excellent humor and with flowers. I had to wait an hour in the living room before she appeared, staggering a bit, grim, in a terrible mood, with a cigarette in her hand.

Pointing a finger at me, she asked: "What do you want from me?"

"Why, I'm Alberto Claudio, the nephew of Tullio Treves. We met a few days ago."

"Ah, that's right. I thought you were somebody else. What can I do for you?"

"I came to say goodbye before going back to Europe, and I would be very happy if you would read me some of those letters you mentioned to me the other day."

"What letters?"

"Why, the letters from Uncle Tullio that have been such a frequent comfort to you . . ."

"I don't know what you're talking about. Don't think you can make me say things I never said! I'm an old woman and I don't like bullying manners in my house. I knew your uncle when I was young: that's all. I think it's proper for you to take an interest in that relative of yours, but don't exaggerate. You're intelligent and can realize on your own that if there were any personal, secret aspects of this story, I wouldn't come to confide them to you! In any case, I advise you not to waste time in a vain attempt to learn the exact circumstances of your uncle's death. Those were times you can't imagine, when there were no truths. Anyone could have betrayed him, for a piece of bread or a stick of firewood! Believe me, I'm not trying to be romantic. You should regret that you never met poor Tullio. But now what can be done?"

"I don't think regret will carry me very far, but I'll bear in mind your advice not to investigate any further."

"In case you were ever to suspect I might be the cause of everything: even if you were right, I wouldn't admit it, and since there is no proof, you'd just make yourself look ridiculous. Now I must leave you, but if you come back to New York, do get in touch. I'd be delighted. Unfortunately, I don't know if I'll go to Europe anymore: travel is expensive, tiring, and everything's changed so!"

"Thanks again for your kindness; I hope I haven't disturbed you too much."

I took leave of Céleste with the same doubts I had had when I left for America. My trip to New York was fruitless. I only satisfied my curiosity, finding out that Céleste does exist and bears a physical resemblance to Thüsis, and that's that! Otherwise, she is an ambiguous person, of volatile moods, and it's impossible to know what she's really thinking.

After that visit, there was nothing left for me to do but return, empty-handed, to Turin. I would, indeed, have been better advised not to waste time looking for things I would never find. Now I was worried about my return. How would Thüsis react, after this futile and too-long trip?

I said goodbye to Bill and Nancy, admitting that Céleste was a dangerous woman, but I thanked Bill for the opportunity to meet her and learn things useful for my research. Happy to hear me tell them what they wanted to hear, they said goodbye warmly, and urged me to take good care of Thüsis.

PART EIGHT

How Reality
Draws Us
into Fiction

20

Returning to Turin sparked unexpected reactions in me. The fact that Céleste had definitively discouraged me from continuing my investigation produced the same sensation of emptiness I had felt years ago, when I got my university degree. All during the flight back questions were churning in my mind: Now what? What should I do with my life? It seemed to me impossible to go back to Thüsis with empty hands. This renunciation depressed me, and everything inside me seemed to rebel. When I arrived at the villa, instead of calming down, I was gripped by powerful agitation. Rapachi came at once to say hello, with great politeness, asking me if I had had a good trip; I answered him curtly. I told him I was tired and would speak to him some other time. In his politeness I thought I sensed something treacherous, and the villa seemed to me a bewitched, dangerous place. I wandered around the empty rooms, then I went out into the garden. I felt the dampness and cold penetrating my bones, I saw autumn coming, the leaves beginning to fall; the garden was sad, and as I was thinking that I should call Thüsis, I felt a storm approaching. So I decided to go to bed; rest would surely calm me. I went to bed without undressing, and, lying inert, I listened to the sound of doors and windows creaking and slamming, I saw the lightning in the sky, I heard the thunder and the rustle of trees whipped by the wind. My room was dark and cold. I didn't want to look for a blanket, and I huddled up, seeking warmth.

What should I do with myself? I was like a sick animal, and to me life seemed a path sown with obstacles and traps that I would never overcome. I sensed the arrival of the storm in an anxious doze. I had the impression that the house, the trees, the bed had started spinning dizzily. If I closed my eyes I could distinctly see Tullio and Céleste, in corso Vittorio, during the air raids. The thunder and lightning became the sound of the airplanes releasing their bombs. In those conditions loving must have been like a hallucinatory drug. What was I doing in that enormous villa? I was there because my mother had died, and, also because my mother had died, I would have to consult more lawyers, go back to Paris, see Aunt Miriam. No, I didn't feel up to it.

I didn't even know where my legal residence was; what taxes I would have to pay; I didn't understand anything. I was a writer, not a businessman. But what kind of writer was I, when it had been months since I wrote a line or conferred with my publisher? Dressed, my shoes on my feet, I thrust myself between the slightly yellowing linen sheets, embroidered with the initials of God knows what ancestor.

The sounds of the storm grew louder and the water fell heavily, implacable. It was something like the Flood and I was in Noah's Ark. I wanted Thüsis with me in those sheets, to make love with her. Her animal way of making love, those exaggerated desires, those coarse words that came from her spontaneously were suited to this shipwreck scenario. We could have indulged ourselves, between the bed and the kitchen, in a way of life progressively damper and colder, where the only stimulus would be the reassuring, animal heat of our bodies.

Rapachi could have provided us with bread, soup, barbera, and nobody would force us to leave that villa. Staying there, like animals without destiny, waiting only for spring to come. Probably in that delirium that would lead us to suicide, we would also experience moments of happiness. That happiness I was sure Tullio and Céleste had experienced in corso Vittorio. No, I couldn't bring myself to call Thüsis to tell her I was back, that I had discovered nothing new, and that Aunt Céleste considered it rational for us to stop our investigation. I could invite her to the movies, we would go and make love in piazza Carignano. But how had I ended up in Turin, in this situation?

The rain continued pouring down furiously, and now the wet panes blocked the view. The windows seemed swollen with steam and you could see only a blanket of clouds rent by lightning.

I couldn't stay there without Thüsis, but Thüsis wouldn't come, and besides the storm would also end, and I didn't want it to end. I felt like a shipwrecked sailor in the storm, but while the storm lasted I would live as if in a spell I didn't want broken. The spell broke before the storm ended, for a not very poetic reason: hunger. I was seized by an outrageous hunger, a precise yearning for bread and butter and Marmite. I desired the salty, acid, and sticky taste of that extract used for making soup or spreading on bread, that soft white bread, always a bit moist, that they eat in England. So I had a piercing hunger and thirst for a warm Guinness, the way they serve it in pubs. With no logical nexus, I saw again my house in London, heard again the good-humored sound of Leonarda's voice, the taste of her coffee, and also the aroma of that dish of roast lamb: that souvla I always ate in a Greek restaurant near the house. It occurred to me that in London, autumn is darker than elsewhere but at least there the lawns remain green.

As my appetite was growing and I saw the storm dying down, I rediscovered a certain inner well-being, as I decided that for the present I would go back to London without seeing Thüsis. I would call her from there, and ask her to join me. I had to find again my old life, emerge from the memory of my mother's death, from the thoughts of Tullio and Céleste and their story. It had been a kind of long vacation, and now I had to go home. And Thüsis? When I saw her again, I didn't want to feel guilty. It was necessary to let some time pass. To find her again without Tullio and Céleste required a pause, an intermission. And so, after a night's sleep, a stroll in the garden with Rapachi, and a few phone calls, I left for London, forcing myself not to call Thüsis.

21

When I arrived in London, I had the sensation that I had come home. The route was the same as always: the airport, the black taxi, the motorway, and the clock you see as you reach Kensington with the FIAT sign, the green lawns, the playing fields, the horses, the blue-gray and violet colors. My studio was cold and damp. On the bed, where I had left it, there was still that copy of *Ulysses* I had started reading during the days before my unexpected departure for Turin.

I opened the house the way you open up the shop after the holidays. There was a lot of mail, mostly bank statements and light bills, gas, telephone. I also found a letter from my publisher asking me why I was so silent. I must answer him as soon as possible, to assure him I'm working on a new book. The phone has been cut off and I can't say, at least from the state I've found the studio in, that Leonarda has been working herself to death. So I can't call Thüsis. Maybe I should write her. I haven't been very honest. She was expecting me in Turin, and I ran away. But I couldn't take that villa anymore; I felt like a ghost. How could I have put Tullio and Céleste aside, when everything around me recalled them?

I went to eat in my usual Greek restaurant: an ugly place in a half-ruined house: a hovel. The owner and his wife made a fuss over me, asking me where I'd been. I chatted a bit with them, ate souvla, and drank quite a lot of retsina. This was my life, my people; these were my places. Coming into the studio, I was pleased to see my clothes again, my papers, my books. These were things that really belonged to me! Immediately I had that feeling you have in London: of being protected and far from everything, of being able to live without schedules. Leonarda's husband answered and told me she wasn't home, but he would be sure to ask her to come by the studio. At Cinderella's house there was the recording. I left a message: "I'm in London. I don't have a phone. Please come by the studio. I'll call you later."

When I came home, I began writing to Thüsis.

Dear Thüsis,

I've come back to London, to deal with a number of things left undone. In New York I saw Aunt Céleste twice. She's a fascinating woman, but I didn't discover anything new. She absolutely denied any possibility that Uncle Tullio could have survived, and she suggested I abandon all my speculations about the how and the where and the why of his being killed, or not. Perhaps I'll be able to explain to you better what happened, when we talk. I've come to London to try to reestablish some order in my life and to start working again. I didn't feel like coming back to Turin empty-handed. For that matter, I have the impression that I'm a burden to you,

and I'd rather you came to see me here. I say
this, knowing I'll have to be the one to
come . . .

I broke off the letter. It seemed banal, saccharine. Then,
in a fury, I took a shower, put on an old blue flannel suit,
knotted a yellow sweater around my neck, and went out
to hunt for a taxi. I had it drop me off in Chelsea, where
I went in and out of various shops and chatted with the
shopkeepers, who spoke with me as if I had never left. It's
strange what faithful friends the English are. As I made
the rounds of those shops, I realized I was there because I
was hoping to run into Cinderella. I would have liked to
see from the distance that too-big behind of hers, those
too-long legs, catch a whiff of her perfume or overhear
her talking with one of those shopkeepers in her show of
fake shyness. I would have liked to catch the tone of her
voice, glimpse a gesture of hers, hear her say "Hi" as if
seeing me were something to be taken for granted, something natural. But since this isn't how things went, I headed
for her house. I didn't see her car. Then I telephoned from
a booth: once again the recording answered. Cinderella
had gone to the trouble of recording her high voice with
a musical background. Even in the recording she was in-
corribly vain. It's odd how nothing has changed. Months
have gone by, and I feel the same agitation I used to feel
then. I am jealous, anxious, I wait for her, I watch to see
if the car appears at the corner. I stand outside number 16,
the house next to hers, where I see lots of people going in
and out, two gentlemen wave to me, the two actors who
live at number 22.
After more than a half hour of speculation and coun-
terspeculation about where Cinderella might be, I decide
to call her friend Ada.

Ada hasn't had any news for some time, and didn't even know that Cinderella was in London. Going back toward her house, I see the car parked awkwardly, one wheel on the sidewalk. Seized by an inexplicable happiness, I rush to ring the bell, twice: our old signal.

The door was opened by a thirty-year-old punk, wearing black leather, his hair dyed pink.

"Anything I can do for you?"

"I'd like to see Cinderella."

"She's on the phone."

In the background a little girl's voice could be heard. In that apartment, which we had furnished with some things of hers and some of mine, everything was changed. It had become an English home, with children, balloons, the smell of bacon, the steady hum of the television, always turned on . . . As I went into the living room I saw that the kitchen had become a normal kitchen, where instead of lovemaking on the floor, the children's meals were prepared according to their school schedules. As I was thinking this, the little girl appeared: the opposite of what I had thought.

Dark, with thick ringlets, pretty. She resembles her mother in the line of her eyes. The thirty-year-old punk stepped aside for me, unaware of my previous status.

At the door, he asked me: "Can you wait a minute?"

I stay on the landing. I wait, the little girl looks at me, without a word, the punk comes back, and says: "Cinderella's still on the phone."

"That's all right. Thanks."

I stand there, but almost immediately I hear a click, and then a bored question, "Who is it?"

"Alberto Claudio."

"Ah, it's you! I got your message. Couldn't you wait? I told you I live with my daughter now."

"And what about the guy in the black leather?"

"He's a friend. He's very fond of me."

"Can I come in for a moment?"

"Not now. I'm busy. But unless I go to Paris, I'll drop by your studio one of these nights."

"When? I need to talk to you. I want to spend a day with you, the two of us . . . I miss you."

"You could have come before, a month ago, when I was here for two weeks all alone. I tried to get in touch with you, and they told me you were in America. You were in high spirits then, but things pass . . ."

The punk came out of the kitchen, waved at me, kissed her on the mouth, and left, saying: "See you later."

"Do you live together?"

"He doesn't have his own place; he stays with me. He's very sweet with Lola."

"How old is he?"

"Twenty-seven."

"He's very young for you."

"He's cute, but now I have to take the child out, and before that I have some telephoning to do. I'll drop by the studio one night soon."

"Will you come tonight?"

"I don't know. I'll phone you."

"They cut the phone off."

"Oh, yes, well, 'bye. See you later. Leave me now and don't just drop in again. I hope you realize the situation has changed."

I left in despair. I was alone in the street, the sky was leaden, my phone was cut off, and she was living with a punk. I had been seized by a wild desire to make love with her in the kitchen, as I had done other times. Her eyes were empty, sated, she moved always indolently and leaned, limp, against the radiator. Her usual ways. Slacks too tight, her blouse just a bit too unbuttoned, pink tennis shoes, and a new brand of cigarette. She was still tanned. Frustrated, I felt alone, and I looked for a taxi to take me God knows where. I felt ridiculous in my proper blue flannel suit, and I envied that punk, who knew nothing about the two of us and spent the night with her. I realized from the way they kissed that she was taken by that boy and that between her daughter and him she had found an equilibrium. The bourgeois aesthetic created by the child's presence was broken by that pale, pink creature who went out without saying where he was going. He was colder, more indifferent, more lacking in emotions than she was. I was succumbing again to the fascination of that feline who would come to my studio: but when? My place was occupied now. And Thüsis? Shouldn't I get in touch with her? For some unknown reason I asked the driver to take me to the Savoy. I was rich: I could go there. I wanted a room with a view of the river and I didn't want to go back to the studio and my old habits. So I took a suite, bedroom and sitting room, then I went down to the street again, bought a newspaper, and began to walk around Trafalgar Square and Covent Garden. A gray, official London. From the hotel I called Cinderella.

"Hello?"

"I'll be waiting for you at the Savoy, after midnight. Have them wake me. Suite two-oh-seven. See you later."

I hung up. It was only eight o'clock; I ordered some sandwiches and a bottle of champagne. I went downstairs, took another walk, then I sat in the lobby to watch the people. I overtipped the porter for the pleasure of seeing his expression change, and then I asked him to send Cinderella up in the event that she came.

I hesitated between writing Thüsis another letter and telephoning her. In the end I called the Pensione Europa, where they told me she had gone out. Exhausted by this day, I took a Valium to relax.

Cinderella came up to the room about one a.m. We ate sandwiches and made love almost without speaking. When she went off, I could already hear the noises of the cleaning staff. At the windows you could glimpse the first colors of daylight. We made love intensely, perhaps because of the situation. What did it matter? As we were making love, I had continued thinking of Thüsis; I missed the violent, young sexuality. Thüsis made love with a huge desire to feel pleasure, she lost her head, couldn't stop. But Cinderella was passive, with little initiative. She always repeated the same phrases, which seemed erotic to her, as if I were the object of her masturbation.

I got drunk two days in a row. I told the porter to say I had left if anyone asked for me. It seemed to me extraordinary to be alone in that huge, slightly dowdy bedroom, or in that lugubrious, damask-walled sitting room; to see the boats on the river, to go down into the streets, always wearing the same suit, the same shirt.

I also would lie for long periods of time in the bathtub, playing with the water. I no longer felt guilty, and I was enjoying myself. All I had to do was press a button and they would bring me anything I wanted, do whatever I asked. I knew I could pay the bill, no matter how much it was, and that independence made me light-headed.

I ordered two cigars, champagne, and a Vietnamese masseuse. My wishes were granted as if I were a sheik. When the Vietnamese girl had left, I took a sheet of stationery and wrote:

My dear publisher,

I break my silence by apologizing for it. I
wanted to write when I had concrete news for
you. I have begun writing a novel that takes
place in Turin during Fascism. The protagonist is
a Fascist Jew, and the book will be written in diary form. I hope to have a first draft finished by
spring. . . . In any case, I'll come and see you
very soon. I haven't written also because my
mother died recently and I had to go to the
States. Many things, in other words, have happened, and I'll tell you about them when I see
you.

Warmest regards.

Alberto Claudio

It was yesterday evening, as I was walking around Char-
ing Cross and then Trafalgar Square. I went into the station
and, in a daze, I started watching the people rushing to
catch trains or jumping off them. Strong odors of petrol,
cold, urine. Mankind in perpetual motion. Smells of coffee
and beer, paint, newspapers. Right there I realized that
Tullio was the protagonist of my novel, still all disjointed
and hazy.

Only this evening, when the Vietnamese masseuse left,
I felt I would solve the riddle of the death or survival of
Tullio Treves through writing. I decided to patch together
the diary and the notebook, and to continue them. So I
will write an imaginary diary. I will put myself in Tullio's
shoes and, assuming that he survived, I will tell what happened to him, in the first person. In this way I'll provide
my explanation of the events, ignoring Céleste's advice.

The thing that stimulates me and amuses me about having him survive is that so many witnesses have expressed varying opinions, always taking his death as something certain, whereas I take as certain his survival.

On Savoy writing paper I immediately set to work, picking up the diary in January 1944.

PART NINE

Writing a Novel

22

Turin, January 1944

I resume writing in a new notebook, and I really don't know what will come from my pen, given my spiritual state. I am in Turin, in corso Vittorio; I am Tullio Treves, I am alive, I am writing in the bath, I am Jewish, Fascist, in hiding . . .

I write this in an effort to contradict, at least in writing, what I discovered a few days ago on reading the newspapers; namely, that I was executed with my entire family in a locality of the Valle d'Aosta. Learning of your own death while you are alive might seem ironic, but to discover that my wife and children died with me is a tragedy. It is a tragedy because, though I might still cherish a slight hope that they are not dead, I can do absolutely nothing to obtain information. If I went to the German or Fascist authorities under the assumed name of Luigi Podda to inquire about the slaughter, I would become suspicious because of my excessive curiosity; and if I were to reveal that I am really Tullio Treves, that I am alive and am investigating the death of my family, the Nazis and the Fascist Republicans, unable to admit having made such a sensational mistake, would kill me or deport me. So I am in my house, now inexorably bound to my identity as Luigi Podda, and I can't even go to see my few remaining friends, who good-naturedly pretend to be unaware of my clandestine life, because otherwise I would cause them serious embarrassment. To say I am desperate is an understatement; a situation like this prevents me from thinking clearly and leaves me dumb. I don't know what to say of this disaster. I felt guilty of having drawn them to that horrible end and doubly guilty because I alone should have been killed. I have been punished by the loss of all identity on earth except for the fictitious one of Luigi Podda. In the very depths of my being I feel shame for not having gone to visit my loved ones, out of weakness and indecision. In the days before the massacre, I was suffering frightful tension, I felt ill-at-ease, not knowing whether the right thing was to stay with C. in Turin or to join my family. In my foolish ingenuousness I would never have imagined that my loved ones could come to such a ghastly end.

I really don't know what to do with myself, and I believe the worst punishment I can inflict on myself is to have to find the strength to survive. I would never forgive myself if I exploited this grief that strikes me in the back to muster the courage to escape with C. In fact, on this day, to honor the memory of those poor innocents, drawn by me to disaster, I make this vow in writing: to have no further relations with C., though I still feel great love for her. The only way to avoid hurting her is to let her believe, as she will have read in the papers, the news of my death. It would be too cowardly to reveal to her that I'm alive and to have to explain to her the moral reasons why I have vowed not to see her again.

I will confess, in these pages, that it is extremely painful for me to make the decision to survive and to try to save myself. Unable to find any justification or solace for what happened, I prefer that my brothers, cousins, and friends should never suspect my survival. The world is large enough so that we need never meet again. But I must work out a way of disappearing.

February 1944

I abandoned the corso Vittorio apartment like an escaping criminal. Not even the maid, Esther Moscati, should find me alive. I could have no witness to my survival. So, with a suitcase of linen and two books, I rushed to Porta Nuova and climbed at random onto the first departing train: Alessandria, Genoa. Along the way I would decide whether to get off at Asti and seek temporary refuge in the country or to go on to Genoa. Perhaps a large city would be more suitable to anonymity.

February 1944

On the train I met a distinguished gentleman, an engineer from Turin, who was going to join his family at Sartirana, a town near Mortara. I asked him what that town was like and if he thought I would find some peasants there who would take me in for a while.

The engineer, a bald man, calmly smoking a cigar, invited me to come to his house, where he could offer me a simple but spacious room.

The house of the engineer and his family is, indeed, very spacious and decent. The room where I sleep is plain, but comfortable; the food is abundant and tasty. I can't remember when I last ate white bread and salted dishes without any limitations. The wine is excellent, and my host and hostess are extremely kind and tactful. I find it very correct of them not to ask why I am here, what my profession is, if I have a family . . .

The people who live in the house are the engineer, who goes back and forth to Turin, his wife, a very refined woman who looks after me considerately, a twenty-year-old daughter, and the grandmother. From time to time a boy also turns up, Piero, who is surely a partisan, but since I have to concern myself with my survival, I can't allow myself the luxury of suspecting him.

I would describe my hosts as a typical good family of the professional class. Mildly anti-Fascist. I could assume the engineer was formerly a supporter of Giolitti, but not fanatically. But this is all guesswork on my part. Now that the first days are past, I ask myself what I'm doing here and how long I should remain. Tullio Treves is dead, and Luigi Podda now has to find a place for himself. I could go to Verona and look up Vittorio Cardin, who was my orderly during the other war. I could explain to Vittorio the situation I'm in, and he would keep silent about it. There are also a number of other trusted persons I could turn to; they would certainly understand my situation and help me, but I'd be running the risk of later troubles. They would end up convincing me I've done nothing wrong and that I should find a hiding place and wait for the war to end, then resume contact with my remaining relatives.

I can't go back on my decision. True, I don't have much liking for this Social Republic, completely controlled by the Germans, but joining it could also be an act of solidarity toward Mussolini.

The ideal situation would be for me to get to see the Duce and explain to him the trouble I'm in. As he's only anti-Semitic for political reasons, he would help me out of this position. One thing is sure: I can't stay here too long — unless I find the courage to tell my host and his wife how things really stand, and they agree to keep me here for a few months and I can begin writing.

March 1944

In the end I compromised myself and told my hosts that I was looking for refuge because, though I am not a partisan, I am wanted by the Germans. I told them I would prefer for them to take my word for it, without asking for further explanations, and that I would pay for my keep with some jewels. They accepted my request with great decorum, saying it wasn't necessary for me to part with my jewels, that another mouth to feed was no problem for them, since we are in the country. I spent serene days, in a sense becoming part of a new family that has agreed so cordially to take me in. I believe I have cheered them up, often playing their old, out-of-tune piano, which hadn't been touched for years. I get on particularly well with the old grandmother. I let her tell me, by the hour, stories from the past. Her son-in-law, the engineer, who comes from Novara, was also an officer in the other war, and when he is here we happily recall that period, which for me was the most beautiful of my life. Though I cannot really treat my wounds and I look toward the future with apprehension, I feel rewarded by the company of these honest and respectable people, with sound principles. It is very relaxing, to become integrated in a classic Po Valley family, because I have a presentiment that sooner or later I will be forced to leave my beloved fatherland. I am determined to emigrate not only because I don't want to be discovered but also because I don't want to know a different Italy, where I wouldn't have even the satisfaction of seeing my children grow up. Having always harbored anti-

American, anti-English, anti-Soviet feelings, hating the democracies, perhaps I will emigrate to Spain or Portugal or Latin America; the prospect is not very inviting. I could turn to the Foreign Legion or even go to live in Palestine; though I've always been an anti-Zionist, too, I could guard my anonymity by going to work in a kibbutz. To be sure, as a Fascist from the dawn of Fascism, it would be humiliating for me to end up in a socialist microcosm, with Polish and Russian Jewish intellectuals!

Try as I will, I can't forget Céleste. I often wonder what has become of her, where she has ended up. Sometimes, at night, I am seized by strong yearnings to go look for her, fling myself in her arms, renege on my vow, and go off with her. This serene condition, as respected guest, though I appreciate it, sometimes weighs on me, and I can't wait to emerge from it. The war seems much longer than I had thought, and the Allies' advance much less rapid than I foresaw. In these conditions time flows slowly, and the more time passes, the more it seems to me terribly unreal and void of meaning. I keep daydreaming about a possible meeting with the Duce. Feeling completely alienated from the Fascist environment is a great burden for me; I feel alone, as my only human contact is in polite conversation about the days of Caporetto and Vittorio Veneto with an elderly lady and an engineer. Piero, the son, doesn't seem trustworthy to me; I find him arrogant, especially when he talks self-confidently about a great new Italian republic. It hurts me to see how today's young people are so different from the way we were. They are less disciplined, braggarts, with little sense of duty or fatherland. To be a partisan nowadays is a sign of opportunism. And to think that this boy, now preparing so boldly a future in an Anglo-American colony, until a few years ago was a student and a member of the Young Fascist

University Students organization. Though I find him dis-
agreeable, in his youth and somewhat harsh good looks
there is also an attractive quality.

I close the notebook in which I am writing in the first
person as if I were Tullio Treves. I am in a state of be-
wilderment. As I wrote, I really felt I was Tullio, and I
seemed to be experiencing the events I was narrating.
But now I must find the way to tell what happens to
him in 1944–45; what will become of him and Céleste? I
feel I should go back to Turin, to consult the newspapers
of the period and to be in the place where my character
lived and moved.

The novel's requirements have precipitated the events
of my life. Before leaving the Savoy, I said a final goodbye
to Cinderella with a laconic phone call, telling her I had
to go back to Italy to deal with my business affairs. She
was equally cold, saying that she hoped to see me again
in six months. She reminded me that I would be better
advised to concern myself with my writing rather than
turn into a *rentier*. I told her I would bear her advice in
mind, and I ended the call by asking her to remember me
to her daughter and to her friend with the pink hair.
I left directly from the Savoy with a supply of writing
paper, without going by the studio and without sending
word to Thüsis. I was going away because I wanted to
have Thüsis read the pages I had written. I had begun the
novel thanks to her, and so I wanted her to feel as if she
had a share in it.
We met in piazza Carignano, only lovers, only a couple
in love, without any stories to tell each other.
We spent sweet, affectionate days in Turin. I went to
the library, she went to class. She asked me absently about

Aunt Céleste and I told her about my trip and I made her laugh till she cried, when I described to her the social, honeyed welcome I got from Bill and Nancy. It was only several days later that the subject of Tullio and Céleste and hence of my book finally came up. In a general way I explained to her what I wanted to write, and she encouraged me, saying it sounded like an interesting idea. Since then, as you might say to certain acquaintances, "Come and have lunch with me one of these days," knowing that nothing will come of it, I often say to Thüsis, "I must read you what I'm writing," and that's an end of it. Actually, my not reading to her drives me to continue writing.

23

2 May 1944

I am writing in corso Vittorio. Three days ago I escaped from Sartirana and after a journey several times interrupted by air raids, I have come back to my apartment.

My life as a guest, as a refugee in the country, had become depressing, precisely because I couldn't have been better treated, never have felt more protected. But why protect yourself when you have nothing to lose? The real motive that inspired my decision to leave was an irrepressible desire to break my vow not to see Céleste again. At the moment when I learned of the death of my loved ones, outrage led me to inflict a punishment on myself. But now I have realized it's too late: if there was guilt, the guilty deed has been done. And now? The events of these past few years have shattered that inner firmness acquired in youth, during the other war, and in the early years of Fascism: a firmness that made me believe totally in my actions and my decisions, because my life was motivated by an ideal. I am not writing this to justify, in my own eyes, the fact that I have sunk to breaking an oath. I am writing this because I am ashamed of having lost all belief in oaths.

So I might as well live like this, spurred by momentary impulses, without any rule.

At Sartirana all that good sense and those good manners made me nervous, bored me. With a war and a civil war going on, since I couldn't fight on one side and wouldn't want to fight on the other, the only thing left was for me to live at least like a man of the city, the daily life of my city, in my house, with all the discomfort and danger that could involve.

And so Cavalier Luigi Podda has come back to corso Vittorio. The apartment is icy, damaged. Luckily, the glass in the bathroom window is still intact, and the electric heater works. I have camped in here, where I am writing and where I have moved everything. Besides the sink, the tub, and the water closet there are a table, two chairs, a little cupboard, and the radio.

At mealtimes I run to the kitchen to light the gas and put the water on to boil, then I go back to the bath. When, according to my calculations, the water is boiling, I run back to drop the rice in it, then I go back to drain it, and I bring it into the bath to eat it. I use my bedroom only to sleep, on a pallet without any mattress.

Domestic chores take up a great deal of my time, also, because I am a hopeless housekeeper. True, I am waiting for Céleste; I hope to run into her, or that she will come here looking for me. Perhaps, feeling nostalgia for this apartment, she will make a pilgrimage here, to weep or to see if some trace has remained, a letter for her. My waiting for Céleste is peaceful, and I feel a certain contentment with the daily life of Turin, so incredibly changed since the armistice. On the one hand, it seems calmer, because the Allies have taken to bombing the city in the daytime and only specific objectives; on the other hand, despite the wretched efforts of the very few remaining Fascists, Turin has become a German colony. On all sides there are signs in German, notices that say "Aufruf," and you hear the loud tread of the occupier's boots.

All the same, the temperature is milder, and spring is coming. There are many refugees, but those who have remained in the city try to leave here in the most normal way possible.

Beyond the horror of awaiting an imminent and certain end, which cannot be expected on any precise date, however, the people live in the constant concern with the lack of food. At Sartirana we ate well; here there is nothing to be found, and it is a struggle to have a scrap of white bread, a bit of meat or salt. Cigarettes are also scarce, and now we have all become used to smoking butts crumbled in rice paper.

24

January 1945

After many months, I am taking advantage of an afternoon when I am alone in the house, in the bath, to note
down some events of this period.

I would say that the cold has become the most serious
problem of the war. The other day, as I was walking in
the snow along corso Re Umberto, I saw that some trees
had been stripped of their boughs, and I don't dare think
of the fate of the trees on the outlying boulevards, in this
scarcity of wood. Turin, especially if you look down from
the hills, looks like a ski resort, and I believe the temperature is hovering around twenty degrees below zero.

I live, clinging to the hope that my electric boiler won't
break down, because that would be a real disaster.

Since my return from Sartirana, I am in the midst of a
situation of constant bustle, because my house has been
transformed into a refuge, and everyone's social life takes
place in the bathroom.

Two young people, Furio and Fosca, are living with me,
and they have changed the living room into a bedroom,
and there is De Feo, an old Fascist companion-in-arms,

who has been hiding in my former dining room since he deserted the ranks of the militia and turned against Salò. De Feo is a man of the Right, and is shocked not so much by the ruin Mussolini has involved us in as by the Duce's "socialist" policy. De Feo doesn't feel he can be a militant Fascist anymore, now that the government includes men like Bombacci, an old companion of Mussolini's socialist battles.

How did these refugee-guests end up in my house?

One Sunday morning last summer, around noon, as I was strolling downtown, I stopped in piazza San Carlo. The square was rather animated, until two truckloads of French "collaborationists" arrived. They got out, carrying musical instruments. The intention of these men was to thank the people of Turin for their hospitality by giving a concert. Unfortunately, the law of terror reigns these days, and the bystanders, terrified by the blue uniforms, scattered from the square in an instant. I, who had nothing to lose, stopped to hear the concert. At the end there was the faint applause from the few people left, and as the collaborationist musicians were putting away their instruments, I heard a voice cry, "Tullio!" I could hardly believe that someone was calling me in the street by my real name. I was no longer used to it, and though I didn't feel any fear, I looked around with some concern and failed to recognize the man in a light brown suit, coming toward me with a friendly manner.

"Treves, don't you remember me? Guido De Feo. Surprised to see me in civilian clothes, aren't you? Ah, well, that's life."

By evening De Feo had already come to stay in corso Vittorio and had set up a cot in the dining room. Since then I talk politics with De Feo when Furio and Fosca are out, or else we play cards or chess. In the house everyone knows everything about everyone else. My guests know that I'm a Jew and a Fascist; De Feo and I know that Furio and Fosca are partisans; Furio and Fosca know that De Feo is a dissident Fascist. So my house is a refuge for traitors and for the betrayed, all living together with great human warmth. I must tell about Furio and Fosca. Those are their partisan names. I have never asked any questions on that score, and they also call me Luigi, pretending not to notice that De Feo calls me Tullio. They moved into corso Vittorio while I was a refugee in Sartirana, and they turned my house not only into their love nest but also into a meeting place for the partisans. Since my return there have been no more meetings, and the two come here only to be alone together. They often make me remember those moments of sublime love that I experienced in this same place with Céleste. Maybe that's why I've fallen in love with them. I have fallen in love because of the natural way I discovered them, by chance, in my bed. Everything among us is unsaid and also sweet. Often when they come back from God knows where, they bring home bread and eggs also for me and for De Feo. I believe they are amused by the paradox of their love, their determined battle for the triumph of democracy, living together with two old Fascists, as if De Feo and I were war parents.

I would never have thought to feel such pleasure in watching and discovering a very young man and woman, tall and dark, giving themselves to each other in such rapturous lovemaking. They don't know that I always watch them through the keyhole. And De Feo is not aware of my voyeurism, either. There are so many things I would like to write about this period, some important, others trivial. One of these is the childish pleasure both De Feo and I feel in listening to Radio Tevere, a Fascist station which constantly broadcasts American music, forbidden by the censorship, with the aim of using sly, ridiculous lures to bring the partisans back to the family hearth. We are amused by the nonsense we hear them say, and the music is even better than on the genuine American broadcasts.

My love for Furio and Fosca is platonic, but it is true love. At times I would like to be with them in the bed and ask: "Tell me who I am. What shall I do with myself?"

My relationship with De Feo, on the other hand, is founded on the solidarity between two desperate men who have lost everything and don't know where they will end up. In Furio and Fosca I see the serenity of those who know their future, who have few doubts, and are still happy to be alive in the world. Barely over twenty, they both know they are not guilty of the past, they know they are fighting on the right side, and also the winning side. They know that soon, thanks to many like themselves, justice will be done, the country will be liberated, and they imagine a rosy, democratic future. They don't talk about old ruins like Mussolini, the king, or Badoglio; they belong to a generation that will have to rebuild the country, new and strong. For them Fascism is the past, ruins, dust; they have only to free the country from the remaining enemies. The fact of being daily in contact with death, knowingly risking their lives, doesn't upset them; if anything, it stimulates them. I believe that their love, even if it would have sprung up anyway in normal times, is fed by an additional strength: that of two young people who, if there hadn't been the war, would have attended university, and who instead, with no distinction of sex, have taken up arms to save their country from the oppression of tyrants.

From the way I talk about it, it would seem I am an ardent supporter of the partisan cause, whereas I am actually on the opposite side; but I admire them, and they carry me back in time. When we young people marched on Rome, to the old supporters of Giolitti and Facta we also seemed a bunch of hotheads, and also to those who simply were the age that I am today.

During these months, I must confess, Antonio has also entered my life, a boy from the south, dark, very handsome, a worker in an armament factory, who comes from time to time to cheer up my nights. De Feo suspects nothing; my room is distant from his, and Antonio always arrives late and leaves at dawn. I have also managed to spend some Sunday afternoons in his garret, not far from here. For Antonio I feel great sweetness and violent attraction. This is the first time in my life that I have met with a boy on a regular basis. Before, it happened rarely, always with different boys, and it was a purely physical matter, with nothing sentimental about it. I know I appeal to him, perhaps because I am a cultivated person, perhaps because my sexual demands are a bit unusual and eccentric. It is odd how, when I am with Antonio, I feel close to Céleste. She would understand. He knows nothing about her, or even about what I feel for Furio and Fosca, whom he considers merely tenants. For that matter, Antonio and I don't talk much; we are simply very happy to spend some nights together. When I ask him what he sees in a middle-aged man, not handsome, overweight, he laughs; he has very white teeth, and he doesn't answer. I know he could vanish from my life at any moment, but I don't think about it, I take things as they come, I live in the present and I am resigned to its precariousness.

What frightens me most is that I feel the end is now imminent; this will be the last winter of war, and I have no doubts as to its outcome. Everything will end in atrocious barbarity and vendettas among Italians, and I know that both De Feo and I would be wise to worry about how to elude the fury of the victors.

It irritates me to think that soon things will be normal again, that reconstruction will begin, and my brother will come back from exile to Turin. I still don't know if Luigi Podda will reveal his secret and will become Tullio Treves once more. I can't much believe in having to lead a normal existence in Turin, going every day to the office, concealing my private life. Tullio Treves, moreover, after the tragedies that befell him, could never live with Antonio in Turin.

De Feo will find his city again, his family, his work; Furio and Fosca will perhaps get married. It's unbelievable how, in this evil period, despite the terrible loss I've suffered, the months have flown by and I have lived through a time of exceptional happiness. It's hard to explain how a man can experience one of the most joyous periods of his life, can feel free as never before, at such a murky moment in history and after so many misadventures. In five years of war, in five years of forced inactivity, of life outside the law, of uncertainties of every kind, I seem to have become another person. To be sure, my conscience sometimes gnaws at me because of the death of my loved ones. If I had heeded Löwenthal's warnings, if I had emigrated with them, my wife and children would now be still alive and serene. A bizarre destiny, mine. Am I an adventurer? A murderer? Am I guilty?

February 1945

It was a sunny and cold afternoon; I remember well that wind that pierced to the bone. I went to see Antonio; he was out, and I left a message: "I'll expect you tonight." I don't know why that clean and glacial cold made me feel like walking, and I headed for piazza Castello. The first warning signs of the twilight were beginning to be perceptible, and I suddenly felt like a hot chocolate, which in these times is replaced by a horrible surrogate that we are rightly made to call "karkadè." So I went into Baratti e Milano, and there, seated alone at a table, was Céleste, smoking and leafing through a paper. I felt a hot flush rise to my head, my heart began to pound, and my legs trembled; it was really Céleste. I don't know why, but I had become convinced she had disappeared with the announced death of Tullio Treves. She belonged to a world that no longer existed and to a corso Vittorio where there was no Furio or Fosca, no De Feo, and to a Turin without Antonio.

The moment I saw her, I realized I loved her the same as always, that she was different from everyone else, extraordinary; that she was beautiful, exciting, and that I wanted only to be with her, speak with her. It seemed impossible that this elegant woman, smoking in slow puffs, with her legs crossed in a way that made anyone desire her but feel too humble at the very thought of approaching her — that this very woman had spent days and nights with me, in my bed.

Now she was there, opposite me, a few steps away. Perhaps I should have given up my karkadè and gone off before she could see me.

I was leaving when I heard her cry, "Tullio!" Her eyes expressed happiness; she was incredulous, frightened, she looked at me wide-eyed, as if it were all impossible; then when she focused her gaze and decided it was really me, she recovered herself and, in a steady voice, said: "Luigi! How odd, to see you here."

I sat down beside her, awkward, yearning to kiss her,

caress her. She, too, yearned for sweetness, and she told me so in the way she moved her hands, the way she came closer to me, then fell back.

"They mustn't see us, nobody must know. You behaved like a pig, and I should have expected as much. You were tired of me, and so when the papers said you had died along with your family, you took advantage and slipped away, just as you would have done now, if I hadn't called you. You look less bloated, and your eyes are more watery than usual. If your complexion is any sign, you're leading an unhealthy life. You give way to all kinds of vice with the excuse that you're persecuted by misfortune and your family was exterminated. Nobody knows that now, finally, you feel free. Admit it: you're only sorry that the war is ending, and everybody will have to go back to his place. I still love you; I suffered too much when I thought you were dead. I realized that when you disappeared an irreplaceable part of myself disappeared as well. Why didn't you try to find me? Why didn't you reassure me?"

"Where was I supposed to find you? How could I? First I was a refugee in the country, and then, in the hope of finding you, I came back to corso Vittorio, where I'm still living. I kept telling myself that perhaps out of curiosity, because of some sentimental nostalgia, if you were in Turin you'd come by there."

"I didn't want to torture myself: that's why I never went back to corso Vittorio. How do I seem to you? Have I aged? Do you still want me?"

"You look divine! I love you. I don't want us ever to be separated again!"

"Oh, that's impossible. I'm still living with the same man, in Milan, very precariously, because, of course, we're committed. The war is about to end, they'll want to settle old scores, there'll be every sort of atrocity. I want to escape all that, and as soon as I can, I'll go to Corsica, and then to Paris. I want to find a house there, go back to studying art history, and meet new people. Tullio, I'm afraid for us; in a moment some of my friends, SS officers, will be coming to meet me here, and I don't want them to see us together. It's the swan song, but we must escape, save ourselves. I'm going back to Milan, but I want to be sure of finding you again, after the war. I'll leave messages for you with the porter of the Bristol, in Paris. Are you sure you still love me?"

"Yes."

"Do you have other women?"

"No."

"Swear you'll come to Paris and look for me, and you'll do everything in your power to find me."

"I swear. But I have to succeed. Wouldn't it be more sure if we ran away together, left now, before it's too late, and hid at corso Vittorio and then tried to get to Paris? Now we're together: let's not part. In times like these it seems madness, like tempting fate."

"No, I can't. Don't even think of it. I'm too involved. I don't have time to tell you; there, they're arriving. Go now. Swear you'll come. The Bristol: don't forget. We're blue angels, creatures full of perversity, and that's why they'll save us. Take heart. Now that I know you're alive, for me, little pudgy Jew that you are, you're like Christ, resurrected. But go away this minute; I can hear their footsteps, those boots."

I went away, holding her hand, letting go of it little by little, allowing it to fall into the void. Both us of were happy to have seen each other again as lovers, and desperate at having to separate again . . .

March 1945

In corso Vittorio everything goes on as before, and nobody knows of my meeting with Céleste. I thought of her as missing, as a distant memory; but I had only to feel her presence, look into her eyes, and know that our destinies are still bound together.

Our story goes on, strong and fragile as always. She wouldn't run off with me; she wants to see me again after the war, in Paris. All this seems like a novel, words uttered in a moment of desperation when you let yourself be carried away by dreams, by phrases. But I know that I really will go there and look for her when the war is over. This means that I will have to leave Italy and that I will make a life for myself in Paris, or God knows where, with Céleste. But in the meantime we have to make sure we survive, and cross the border. On the one hand, this project gives me hope; on the other hand, it makes me realize what I'll lose, the fact that Antonio, Furio, Fosca, and De Feo will soon go out of my life, just as corso Vittorio will disappear.

We will find food, goods in the shops again, and our nights will no longer be governed by the curfew. I can't even imagine how I could resume a normal life, a family life, if Allegra and the children weren't dead!

There was a time when it was all different, I believed in the fatherland, in its destiny, I was sure that by working for Mussolini and the Fascist cause I would contribute to Italy's resurgence, its rise to the rank of a great nation. But now! All I see is ruin. Looking at some recent photographs of the Duce taken in Salò, De Feo and I were, in fact, saying that he seems to have become a different person. Humiliated by the Germans, suffering from his ulcer, oppressed by defeat, he has become a puppet. And yet as long as he is alive, the fatherland will have a historic leader!

De Feo says, "All right, now Mussolini is still alive. But then what? It seems incredible that men like De Bono and Ciano were killed with the Fascists' consent. Balbo is dead. Grandi and Bottai have probably gone abroad. The king has betrayed the country, and so has Badoglio. When the war's over, the Anglo-Americans or the Communists will rule, and the king will also come to a bad end. Just wait. It's a hard thing, to be middle-aged, and to see nothing in front of us but the rubble of everything we fought for."

If I follow Céleste to Paris, it means another clandestine adventure. Living in Paris as an exile, with a perverse and mysterious woman, in a hotel . . . I love Furio, Fosca, Antonio, but they think of the future as a new, clean avenue, where their values will triumph; they feel that their generation will restore life to the country, and they will be protagonists. This wearies me, bores me; I prefer anything to reconstruction. I enjoy these ephemeral moments because in them I find true equality, true humanity. Of course, we are living in a tragic period, but it is also strong from a human point of view, and in some ways, truly beautiful. We help one another survive; situations of forced cohabitation have arisen, but with real affection. In corso Vittorio I talk, play cards, laugh, and share scant food with a homosexual, a Fascist, and two partisans. Tomorrow, when democracy begins its progress, we'll go back to egoism, individualism, and each of us will shut himself up inside his own ego.

I'm writing in the bathroom, where I'm still fairly comfortable, but outside the cold is fierce, merciless. I'm waiting for Antonio. I'm alone in the house. Furio and Fosca have gone to the mountains, and De Feo is sleeping at Marta's house.

Poor De Feo would also like to let himself be carried

along by the current and not think of tomorrow. As the months pass he has become fond of his double life between corso Vittorio and Marta's house, but since both he and she are married, they know that soon they will have to go back to their families. I really think that all of us are traitors to some extent, and this common betrayal creates a true brotherhood. In any case, all of us share the fate of having to face constant physical discomfort and, above all, the fact of constantly living in the vicinity of death, amid shelling and air raids. We have become accustomed to the idea that every time we say goodbye, it might be forever. A trifle would suffice, and any one of us could be killed in the street, betrayed, deported.

If I were a real writer, I would like to describe in more precise detail this icy winter, in which fear and gaiety alternate continually.

April 1945

I have remained alone with Antonio. The others have gone, and now he can live freely with me. It won't last long, perhaps only a matter of weeks. Yesterday the city seemed to have gone crazy. A general strike was proclaimed, and the local inhabitants started driving trams at random, not always managing to cope. Turin was like an anthill that had been kicked over; the Turinese played with the trams as if they were carousels.

Furio and Fosca left one morning for the mountains and since then there has been no more news of them.

This sort of disappearance can mean a change of zone of operations, or death, arrest, concentration camp. For days I've waited for them to come back, trying to think of optimistic explanations. Now I've decided that they must have changed zone, and so I won't be able to find out anything about them for a long time. De Feo and I were avoiding the subject, until one day he finally asked me: "Do you think they've been killed? Or deported? Did you know anything about their families? Do you think it'll be possible to meet again after the war?"

I didn't answer him, not that he was expecting an answer. At this point he was very low: Marta had gone and our life together was becoming oppressive. He never left the apartment, thus creating great difficulties also in my life with Antonio; but the worst of it was that, as we were continually together, each of us made the other feel his irresponsibility more acutely. We knew things were getting more dangerous all the time, and the only sensible thing to do was run; but if we lingered, there was no point in constantly torturing each other. De Feo would warn me, stay with me for hours in the bath, unshaven, his eyes tired, as he smoked foul-smelling cigarettes. He said we would end up like rats crushed under the rubble. He felt besieged by enemies who would come and get us, take us through the streets, shaming us; we would be stripped naked, then shot.

He said we would end up like those sides of meat hanging in butchers' shops or as prey for vultures. At times, his eyes wide, wearing his overcoat, he would enter my room in the middle of the night, and wake me up in order to say to me: "Get dressed. We have to act fast. We must go and turn ourselves in to the German authorities," or else, "We have to deny everything and try to join the partisans," or else, "Let's set off and see what happens . . ."

De Feo, too, went out one morning and hasn't come back. I don't know what he did, whether in a delirium he went and turned himself in, or rejoined his family. To be sure, if it weren't for Antonio, I would feel totally alone, desperate.

But instead, Antonio, always affectionate, smiling, and indifferent to outside events, is able to reassure me. He doesn't expect anything from the end of the war. Nothing better, nothing worse. He is an unskilled laborer, and the only change he can foresee in his life with the war's end is that the armament factory will be changed into a tool factory — a change that won't alter his work. What surprises and fascinates me in him is his smile, his tranquillity, his passivity. He seems always in a good humor, glad to be with me. Perhaps he also knows that things will end between us, that one of these days I will have to disappear, like De Feo; but he doesn't talk about it. I have never gone through an emotional relationship in this way. I ask myself how it is possible really to love someone without worrying, without constantly asking questions, without trying to imagine the future.

There are certain nights when he plays with me and makes me forget everything, and then, in the morning, with no sign of weariness, without an alarm clock, he gets up, pulls a blanket over me, and goes off to work. He doesn't even say "See you this evening" or "See you later."

He goes out, I believe, with the certainty of finding me again. His only comment on the disappearance of the people who were living in my house was: "All the better, now we can see each other every evening, earlier, and we won't have to hide."

Antonio lives with his homosexuality naturally, without any feelings of guilt. This, too, the fact of being different, semi-outlaws, is something we never talk about. He tries first and foremost to be sweet and calm with me. He never asks me why I don't work or what I do or why I leave the house so seldom. He expresses no curiosity, but considerately brings to me every evening a piece of white bread he's found God knows where or some cheese or a bit of salt. At night we lie awake for long hours smoking and listening to the radio. But even though I am comfortable, and feel myself tenderly cared for by a loving young person, I live in a state of constant apprehension and am unable to relax. I would like to be able to abandon myself completely to love and its consequences, whatever they may be. I would like to be able to ignore outside events completely and tell myself that I'll be lucky if I just survive. Instead, I torment myself, because I know I should leave, should abandon my room and my bath, escape to Paris. My destiny will be neither Turin nor Antonio. I must join Céleste in Paris. Tullio Treves can't abandon himself to oblivion. Time and again I would have wished a bomb to strike the house and kill us in our sleep or as we lay on the bed, naked, smoking, wrapped in blankets.

All my life I have fought against leaving the fatherland: this obstinacy of mine caused the murder of my loved ones. But now there is no choice. I let myself go in endless walks through the streets of a Turin now springlike, waiting for the imminent liberation, a city that hates the Germans and is preparing to welcome the Anglo-Americans. I walk along the arcades, torn with melancholy, and I sing "Giovinezza" under my breath. I look at this city, which I am not sure I will ever see again, with infinite yearning, wanting at all costs to photograph its image within me. When the weather is clear, I linger to look at the Alps, my beloved Monviso, or else I go to the Po embankments and I can barely restrain my tears. Before having to leave everything, I'd like to go back to our neglected, looted villa, see if Rapachi is still there. At times I tell myself I'm crazy. Actually, nobody is forcing me to run away, and I could very well remain in corso Vittorio and wait for my brother to return from exile.

I could clear up the mystery of my presumed death and start living again, without having to go away from Turin to who knows what other place. But then I console myself, saying that Paris is a city I've loved since childhood, that I'll be able to visit the Louvre, see my favorite pictures.

And yet it isn't easy for someone who for years was a sincere nationalist to have to leave. I am leaving also because I think that there would be no understanding between me and the people I used to see. There's no knowing what experiences my friends have had, living through the war in other countries. They will come back here with the desire to import habits they've learned elsewhere. Our country will change under the influence of these people. What will I do with myself in Paris? Will I find Céleste again? I don't want to end up under the protective, paternalistic wing of my brother-in-law Löwenthal. How can I explain all these things I am writing down to Antonio, asleep in the next room, apparently serene, who loves me and can't remotely imagine all my perplexities?

25

Nice, January 1946

I didn't write any more because I was tormented by doubts. Leave Antonio in order to find Céleste? Go away before or after the end of the war? I didn't want to see the war's end, but at the same time I did want to. Mussolini, killed at Dongo and hanged with la Petacci in piazzale Loreto. Our country filled with neo-American ways, the smell of Camels, wild dances, handsome Negroes in the streets of Turin. Gaiety and the last shots. My days dragged on in corso Vittorio. I learned that De Feo had reached home safely, while poor Fosca was killed near Bra, and Furio has moved to Rome. Antonio was enjoying himself in that atmosphere of newborn peace, and most of all, he was happy because he could buy American clothes. He got himself a crew cut and began swaggering a bit like a cowboy. Antonio's American ways saddened me and cheered me at the same time. Now I had to decide whether to remain Luigi Podda and go away or find Tullio Treves again. The desire to remain Podda, at least temporarily, prevailed. If I had chosen Antonio instead of Céleste, I would have had to suggest he come with me. I had thought that a country where we could take refuge without his suffering too much would be Argentina. I told Antonio I had to go abroad for some years, and I suggested he come to Argentina with me. Curiously, in his reply I seemed to find myself again as a young man. He thanked me, but he said that he would never leave Italy and Turin and he wanted to stay with his mother. We could write, meet during vacations, and if we still loved each other, we would be together again on my return.

I felt I had to go away, even if leaving Antonio grieved me very much. I was in love with him and I was also jealous of him. I suspected he was having some kind of affair with a young black MP who procured clothes and food for him. Through the trivial sexual tie between Antonio and that American I had forgotten my age, my past; and feeling young, I was caught in the trap of reconstruction.

Fate is strange! As I was about to sink, irresponsibly, into a postwar Luigi Podda, not interested in politics but concerned with boogie-woogie and American boys, in piazza San Carlo I was greeted with great cordiality by the Duke of Pistoia, my onetime friend and comrade-in-arms. With the tone typical of the royal family and the Pinerolo cavalry school, he said: "My dear Treves, we must meet, take up the piano again. It's been years since we last saw each other. Let's have lunch at Il Cambio one of these days. Goodbye, dear Treves."

Fascism, the racial laws: everything had been erased and forgotten; we spoke of the Resistance, the horrors of the concentration camps were discovered, and Turin was becoming more or less the same as before. And just as the Duke of Pistoia had been unaware of my death, so many others would be the same, and I would easily find a role. But I wanted the caresses of Antonio, of the American soldiers; I wanted to go on living day by day, without work and commitments, without thinking. Antonio's body became more necessary to me every day, and I enjoyed punishing myself, wondering what his black lover was like.

And Céleste? I missed her, too; if it was Antonio's body and youth that attracted me, with Céleste it was her personality, her words, her imagination that held me. I missed some of her gestures, artificial and natural at once, certain vulgarities, certain elegances, certain madnesses in which the body, though reduced to a piece of meat, is still a piece of meat accustomed to European cities, to music, perfumes, journeys, drugs. It excited me to know that I made her feel pleasure because she found my blue eyes too pale, and because she considered both my double chin and my cologne indecent.

Without really knowing what I was doing, I collected some money, which I had hidden out of prudence, a few old boxes and jewels, and left a note for Antonio, then went to Leghorn, where I knew a shipowner, a trustworthy and fine person. He found me a clandestine boat and enabled me to land in Nice, a few days before Christmas.

I live in the pension, where they treat me with respect and where I am bored to death. I think I did the wrong thing, leaving Antonio, and I am in despair because I keep sending telegrams to the Bristol for Céleste and I receive no reply. I live here with my homesickness, and the seafront and the palms sadden and nauseate me. It's too soon to go to Paris: Céleste won't arrive for at least a year. Assuming she is rid of her Fascist, she will have to have found a way to leave and, as she told me, go to Corsica. In the meantime I'll go to Switzerland to get an evaluation of what I managed to bring with me and also to see what my father left for me in a certain bank in Geneva.

Unlike my brother, sincerely believing in Italian self-sufficiency, I always refused to pay any attention to those emergency funds my father created for me. But now it's time for me to give them some thought.

Geneva, July 1946

I'm sitting at La Perle du Lac, about to go off to the mountains with an Argentinian boy I met here in Geneva last month.

To my great surprise I discovered that the capital left me by my dear papa, plus what I managed to bring with me, would allow me to live quite comfortably, without working, for a number of years.

I can't say I'm extremely rich, but sufficiently well-off not to have to worry about material matters. I still have no news of Céleste, whereas I've received a very sweet letter from Antonio, who can't join me for a vacation and tells me he has a crush on an American.

It's strange how things have changed since I've been here in Geneva. After years of physical and moral confusion, fears, dangerous pleasures, after having been reduced to living without a name or a family, after seeing my ideals collapse, now my spirit and my mind respond in a curious way to the present.

Swiss tranquillity, a certain order, a certain regularity in my meals, certain hours and good habits have freed me from the perverse taste of that Babel that Turin had become. Being a refugee here is a natural condition, which doesn't make me feel any different from many others. I am feeling new sensations: the well-being of knowing I have a secure fortune, the closeness to nature, the lake and the mountains, and the way I have spontaneously accepted my homosexuality. Actually, I am glad to go and spend a month in the mountains with a younger man.

I enjoy the way he speaks French with that very distinct accent South Americans have, and even if our relationship isn't a great passion, we are friends and we have kindred tastes: opera, mountains, nature. This situation, without past or future, rests my overstrained nerves and reawakens my awareness. Going to the mountains, I know I will rediscover the joy of clean air, those sometimes violet-gold twilights, those peaks; and at the same time, I will think again of my wife and my children. It's not my fault I didn't die with them; it was chance, not my cowardice. Perhaps I should have realized that my ideals were far less important than my family's survival, but at the time I didn't think that, and in any case I was convinced that none of us would die because I was sure Fascism would triumph in the end. Today I don't even feel any desire to go back to Italy. They have held a referendum; it wasn't enough to slaughter Mussolini and his collaborators, to pretend that no Italian was ever a Fascist; now they have chosen also to force King Umberto to go into exile. As the house of Savoy leaves Italy, it seems to me that I am an exile forever from a country that has chosen to be another country, because of its inability to go on living with certain responsibilities. They have chosen tabula rasa, and anyone who wasn't too openly a Fascist or a monarchist will be able to find a place easily in the new political system. All this disgusts me.

After this holiday I'll decide what to do, whether to go to Paris and look for Céleste or remain here.

Geneva, end of November, 1946

I have learned that my brother has gone back to Turin, believes I am dead, has taken possession of the villa, and has decided to live half the time in America and half in Turin. I know that he has had a daughter and that my presumed death and the deaths of Allegra and the children have been categorized as a tragedy and added to the list of Nazi-Fascist horrors. I have also learned that my Löwenthal sister has returned to live in Paris with her husband and their daughter Miriam and that for them everything is again as it was before.

So I am officially and tragically deceased; I am Luigi Podda, and I have decided to go to Paris. My life as a well-off *rentier* in Switzerland has served me as a convalescence, but I want to join Céleste in Paris. I'm curious to find out how she escaped the war and what our relationship will be. Of course, I sometimes feel a strong homesickness for Antonio, for those raving conversations with De Feo in the bathroom, and I am still mourning the death of Fosca. I would like to see De Feo again, and Furio . . . Antonio is something else: for me he will remain an indelible memory of sensuality, peace, and sweetness. In Paris I must avoid the Löwenthals.

Paris, March 1947

I extended my stay in Switzerland in order to pass the Christmas holidays in Arosa, skiing with Luis. It was very beautiful. In Geneva I resumed playing the piano, practicing every day with an extremely stern Polish lady. Now I have been in Paris a week, but I'm afraid it's only a temporary arrangement. I had to give up the idea of the Lutetia for fear of being recognized, and I remembered a hotel where some Italian friends used to stay, the Lotti, rue de Castiglione. I hear that the Louvre is about to re-open, and I will have time to look at some pictures at my ease. The Bristol has no news of Céleste; at this point I inquire every week, out of habit, but I have a presentiment that she will come back only in autumn. Living at the Lotti depresses me; this seems a neighborhood where I could encounter people I know or even run into my sister, and that would really be the end. On the other hand, I prefer living here to Switzerland. I go to an occasional concert and I have made friends with a doctor, Rudy, a Czech refugee with whom I play cards every now and then.

He is a morphine addict and I must say that, having tried it a few times, I think that if I weren't careful, I might become addicted myself. I also spend some time at jewelers', trying to sell the jewels and boxes I brought with me, and in this Rudy is a great help. It's incredible the way some central Europeans are extraordinarily sensitive to beautiful things.

Luis has come to see me. He has put on weight and seems out of place in Paris.

Late April, 1947

In a few days many things have changed. Going to see a doctor off the boulevard Raspail, I passed the Lutetia, where they have just about finished repairing the wartime damage, and I felt a great pang of nostalgia for that ugly hotel. Though I can never go back to the Lutetia, I realized that if I want to go on living in Paris anonymously, I'd be better off in that neighborhood than in the one where I'm living now.

Of course, the arcades of rue de Rivoli and rue de Castiglione gave me the illusion of old Turin habits, but at that moment it wasn't Turin I was looking for; and besides, I know that those are Russian arcades and the Tuileries garden is a Russian garden. For some unknown reason, I suddenly realized this is April, the last "r" month before September; the oyster season was coming to an end, and all this time I've been in Paris, I've forgotten to eat any. It was evening and I had an immediate desire for a dozen Belons. I walked up the Champs-Elysées, dazed by the traffic noises; and walking as usual at a brisk march, filled with the euphoria of my craving for oysters, I started singing "Giovinezza." From avenue Wagram I arrived at the Brasserie Lorraine.

The moment I sat down, I happened to see a man wearing a beret, haggard face, intelligent look, eating oysters with a carafe of red wine in front of him. I saw he was reading an Italian magazine. "You're Italian?" I asked him openly.

"Yes. Why?"

"I realize that your nationality doesn't entitle me to disturb you and speak to you, but I thought that the fact of your being here probably means you're an oyster enthusiast, like me, and I was curious to know why you drink red wine with them. I've always drunk a dry white, and this variation interests me. Please pardon my curiosity."

The dark man with gray-streaked hair, a long nose, and one of those Italian faces of an irregular beauty that appeals to women, began laughing heartily, like a boy.

"What a fuss! I didn't realize oysters could be so important. I don't dislike them, and since I was nearby and was hungry, I ordered some. The house red is because it costs less, and I hardly ever drink white."

"Pardon me, all the same. You were reading, and I don't mean to interrupt you. I'm surprised that you read Italian papers. I've stopped: it's strange, how Italy has gone out of my life."

"But it hasn't gone, as you see. It always comes back. Being an Italian or a Jew or an artist is something that never leaves a man. Are you here on a business trip?"

"Do I look like a businessman to you?"

"Not particularly. You look like someone who used to be a businessman and now isn't one anymore. You live in Paris?"

"I have been living here for a few months."

"Will it bother you if I light a cigar? You must excuse me, but I'm also curious by nature. You're here for work?"

"No, I don't work. I'm waiting for a lady, who should join me before autumn."

"Why don't you live in Italy?"

"It would come naturally for me to reply in a rude way: and what about you? But I can answer without any embarrassment: I'm in voluntary exile. If I had just been a Fascist, you might think I was escaping, but I am also a Jew, and what's more I live under a false name because in Italy they think I was killed along with my family. And so, instead of being 'the ghost who returns,' I've moved to Paris. I spend my time between the Louvre and the piano. I should live in a safer neighborhood because I have a sister in Paris I don't want to meet."

"My name is Amedeo Recanati, I'm a painter, and I've lived in Paris since it became impossible to live in Italy, around 1925. Now that they've hanged Mussolini and gotten rid of the king, I could even go back; for that matter my comrades want me to go back, but I can't leave Paris at this point. I have a daughter, a former wife, a woman, my habits. I do things for the party from here, as I always have done. I go to Italy in September and stay till All Souls'."

"What do you mean, life in Italy became impossible in '25? That was the glorious beginning of the Fascist Era!"

"It was that glorious beginning that drove me out! I come from a family of anarchists, and I then became a Communist."

"I understand. But now you could go back."

"I told you: I'm too lazy, and besides, everybody turns up here. But you! You should go back to Italy and join the Communist party. Where are you from?"

"Turin."

"City of Gramsci, Togliatti, Pajetta. You could do good work in the party."

"Don't be absurd. I told you: I'm a Fascist and therefore profoundly anti-Communist."

"Togliatti has opened the party to many former Fascists. Honest people whose ideas have changed. Take an artist like Sibilla Aleramo."

"I've come here to meet a woman, who's also a Fascist. She and I want to start a new life."

"You told me you wanted to change hotels. If you'd be content with a modest but pleasant place, I know one near the Luxembourg, not far from my house. Life there is simple; it's like a village. Unfortunately, in this postwar period, with existentialism and the Saint-Germain cafés, the atmosphere has been spoiled a bit. The neighborhood has become fashionable, but it's still nice to live there. Come and see me at my studio one of these afternoons and we'll talk about it. You said you go to the Louvre often. What sort of painting interests you?"

"Géricault, Delacroix."

"Come and take a look at my work. I'll introduce you to some comrades, too. It's funny, meeting a Fascist given up for dead, now eating oysters. I like to see you eating them with such greed and sensuality. You look like a man who would have proper table manners; but you eat with a greediness, as if they were going to snatch your plate away. Anyway, don't get me wrong: all Italians, the minute they get to Paris, want oysters! So I'll be expecting you — six, rue Monsieur le Prince. Come in the afternoon; I'm always there between three and seven. I'll be glad to see you."

"I'll definitely come, and I'll ask you to show me that hotel you mentioned. But I have to know something important: can I bring along my piano, and can I play it?"

"I think you can."

June 1947

For some months I have been living in a little hotel in rue de Tournon. So I live between the Latin Quarter and Montparnasse, and in addition to playing the piano, I spend long hours in cafés. Recanati has drawn me there; ever since our first meeting he has come into my life, a bit the way De Feo did. I have a cat, very cute; I've named him Ignazio. He is very sweet and is good company. I read a lot of historical novels, erotic stories, and sports magazines.

Recanati lives with Jeanne, a likable woman, and he has a daughter, Libera, eighteen, pretty, who studies and can cook spaghetti very well. I have also become very friendly with Titina, his ex-wife, who translates for various French publishers. Titina lives in Montparnasse and hardly ever leaves the quarter. It doesn't bother her that after the period of the "lost generation" those cafés have become places visited by tourists, like the Eiffel Tower. She eats her sandwich of "rillettes et cornichons" and drinks half a liter of red. She is an intelligent woman who always speaks very affectionately both of Amedeo and of Jeanne.

Libera, I would say, is a strange mixture of Amedeo and

Titina. She has acquired her father's laziness and her mother's profundity. There's no telling really who Amedeo is. He paints a picture when he feels like it; otherwise he is all friends and the party. It seems to me that Titina is a much more serious Communist, but she and I talk often about music. For her Bartók is the only composer, and she disapproves of my banal Wagnerian tastes.

Recanati, on the other hand, has insisted on painting my portrait. He keeps on saying I should join the Communist party and if I don't feel like going back to Italy immediately, I could do good work for the party in Paris. At the insistence of Amedeo and Titina, I am reading books on Marxism, and I realize I feel a strange liking for Stalin and Togliatti. Probably Togliatti would be able to give Italy again that discipline the country needs. But it would be absurd for me to become a militant Communist. For the present in Italy the Communists have to collaborate with the democratic system, and it is democracy, precisely, that I don't believe in.

I think I will go and spend the holidays in a village in the Pyrenees with Recanati; and from there I'll take a little trip into Spain.

Perhaps that's the country where I could settle. Franco has an iron hand and controls Spain well. In Paris I feel a bit weary, with my little morphine games and all these neo-ideologies . . . I really need a holiday.

Madrid, August 1947

I'm at the Ritz, splendid hotel; and I go to the Prado, become lost among the pictures, and I think the Prado is a museum that comes closer to perfection than the Louvre.

Recanati was a good fishing companion for a part of the vacation in the Pyrenees, but the endless debates about the

229

party between him and Jeanne began to tire me in the end.

To learn if I am really attracted by Communism, I should go to Italy. But I keep thinking it's ridiculous; I am an officer, I belong to another world.

Luckily Luis has come to join me, and he is with me here in Madrid. A bit thinner, he is making a great effort to win his diploma from the Geneva conservatory. This perhaps isn't the best moment to visit Spain; actually, I am counting the days, because I feel that my whole life is suspended until Céleste's arrival. On the way back Luis and I stopped at San Sebastian; the place seemed beautiful to me, but sinister, full of light, food, people. In Madrid I went for the first time to a corrida, and I felt great fear. Physical fear, when the bull entered the arena. I clung to Luis, trembling; I wanted to run away. But then the twirling of the capes, the swords, the colors and the staging overcame my fear. The toreros as men don't interest me much. In their exhibitionism there is something that irritates me, because their costumes are too tight and too gaudy.

Luis would like me to go with him next summer to Argentina. He says I would feel at peace over there. To me it seems too remote a country, but a year is a long time, and I'll have leisure to think it over.

Paris, 3 September 1947

No messages at the Bristol, so I went on to Libera's house, where I found Titina. She brought Ignazio back to me. From the sweet way she spoke of that cat with me, I realized I would make her happy if I gave him to her. I'm sure I have done Ignazio a good turn. I know I'll miss him, but I also know that Céleste can't bear cats, and I prefer not to create occasions of conflict.

Libera is going to Rome to study; she leaves next week. She asked me if I would come and see her and — I don't know why — I said yes.

In that yes there was a basic truth. To see the capital again, after all these years, would be moving, and I would also like to look up Furio.

A few days later I received a letter from De Feo, complaining about his family life and about his work. He thinks the provinces are hopeless, and the MSI — for all its pious Fascism — is a pointless party, empty. De Feo writes that he has seen Furio, who has apparently become an important figure in the Communist party and is close to Togliatti. Since Furio is in Rome, I thought to write him a letter and have Libera deliver it. Maybe, in my unconscious, I imagined that a love story could develop between them. If the dead watch us, I think Fosca would be pleased.

29 September 1947

Céleste has left word at the Bristol that she will arrive in Paris on October 21 with the wagon-lits from Marseilles. She wants me to meet her train at the Gare de Lyon.

Paris, 25 October 1947

Céleste got off the train, thin and tanned, her hair cut short; she was bundled up in a dark coat. She was carrying a little crocodile case, and a porter followed her with a huge trunk. She appeared like a scene in a film. She was very beautiful; her blue eyes seemed darker, her cheekbones more marked. On her little finger she was wearing a ruby in a gold setting, slightly loose.

"I want a croissant and some coffee. You're so pale! Are

you ill? Your hair is curlier than usual. Is it always this cold in Paris?"

Since I saw her at Baratti's in Turin, she had changed. Her manner was a blend of bullying and sweetness, scorn and simplicity. She asked me to stop the taxi at a café, where she ordered two coffees and some croissants.

"I'm happy to see you. We made it, didn't we? We're together again, in Paris. My officer joined the Foreign Legion, I wandered around Italy awhile, and then I spent almost a year on Corsica, partly in our old house, partly at the sea. After all those rotten years I need to purify myself. How do I look? Too tan? Old?"

I don't know why, it wasn't what I thought (I was spellbound by her beauty), but still I replied: "Obscene."

The word put her in a good humor; she wasn't expecting it. "Same old swine. So I see you haven't changed! Why don't you tell the driver to leave my trunk at the Bristol, and then we can go and stroll along the Seine? I haven't been to Paris for years. How do you like it here? Where do you live? What do you do? My God, we have so many things to tell each other!"

We walked for hours: the Seine, Notre-Dame, the Louvre, place de la Concorde, and finally the bar of the Bristol. Céleste allowed the hours to pass, in a lighthearted lingering, because she wanted our bodies to grow to desire each other naturally.

Then we spent a week in the room at the Bristol, where there was only play and passion.

I introduced Recanati, Jeanne, and Titina to Céleste. She found them "petit-bourgeois," boring.

"I don't know how you could have got involved with those failures, those second-rate exiles. And that Titina, with her revolting cat, Ignazio! I hate people who talk about animals as if they were human beings."

232

"I believe my friendship with them was due to my homesickness for Italy."

Paris, April 1948

With the help of drugs, Céleste and I, between the Bristol and my hotel, experienced a frenzied erotic life. Sleepless nights and days were followed by days when we had run out of narcotics or when we swore we would quit. Those were nervous, gloomy times. Our talk became dramatic, repetitive, heavy. Hours of somnolence alternated with hysterical scenes or nausea. We were in Paris, and we were asking ourselves where we should go and live. Several times I suggested Spain, but Céleste considers it provincial. She also dismissed the idea of Argentina, because she is sure it must be a desolate, empty country. If we were ever to leave Paris, she would prefer to settle in London or the States.

When I told Céleste that an Argentinian friend of mine has invited us to spend the Christmas holidays in Switzerland, she asked me, aggressively: "Who is he? Your lover?"

"No, he's an Argentinian friend who is studying music in Geneva; I met him while I was there, just after the war. He's very cultivated, well-mannered, and he likes the mountains."

"Where does he want us to go?"

"Saint Moritz. A hotel there."

So we set off for Switzerland, nervous, without drugs; but Céleste promptly felt at home in that grand hotel atmosphere, that mountain resort where the tone was *d'avant guerre*.

Céleste seemed to bloom; she was made for holidays and luxury. She felt at ease in society, among elegant peo-

233

ple. She immediately made friends with various people staying in the hotel. In the morning she went skating or skiing, she played cards in the afternoon, and at night she wanted to dance till dawn.

I soon realized that in society she was ashamed of me, of my ugliness, and for this reason she tolerated the presence of Luis. She believed that our apparent ménage à trois gave us an aura of elegance and mystery.

Coming back to Paris was difficult. To give some order to our life and show that our love was happy, we decided to look for a house, and this problem immediately began to dig a furrow between us. Céleste wanted to live like an ambassadress or a duchess, and I, like a hermit. We lapsed into using drugs again and, since I preferred morphine and she, cocaine, this was no help.

She believed the normal thing would be for us to move into a circle of aristocrats and gamblers, Germans, middle Europeans, and Scandinavians, whereas I would have liked to see Amedeo, Jeanne, and Titina more often. She despised that kind of intellectual or "failed" artist, and found my talk of Communism frivolous and quite eccentric.

I didn't want a house because I didn't want to settle definitely in Paris. I realized that for Céleste politics was a closed subject and that she would therefore try to bring me together again with the Löwenthals. If the Löwenthals and Céleste were to meet, they would feel they belonged to the same world. So I was afraid that Céleste would soon want me to return to the family, as Tullio Treves. Being Tullio Treves meant resuming a role in society.

I meet Recanati or Titina secretly, when Céleste is playing cards or has gone to the hairdresser. Talking with them does me good, but then it makes me suffer, because it increases my inner disgust with the life I lead with Céleste. Living like this, I squander my money, no longer find time to play the piano, and I feel I should look for a job. But what job? Where? Everything inside me seems to rebel, and I find the basic principles of Marxism justified. So I can no longer consider myself seriously. It seems to me impossible to lose Céleste, and at the same time I feel a desire again for a boy like Antonio, handsome, young, and sweet with me.

Luis writes me often and tells me that he is about to receive his diploma. He wants to go back to Argentina, and is sure it would do me good to join him because there I would find myself again, whereas in Paris I am losing myself over a woman who is not right for me. Paris has become an obsessive maze in which I feel imprisoned and from which I see no avenue of escape. Céleste has found an apartment, and according to her we could be happy in it. I see that place as a symbol of a chain I will never be able to shake off. She says I'm ill, and I need to reflect. She has threatened to leave me, because I can't go on being so unstable, and I should give her a normal life. I should leave my ghosts and find a job.

Paris, 15 May 1948

In the *Figaro,* and then in other papers, which I read to check on the news, yesterday the birth of the State of Israel was proclaimed. The Jews have returned to Jerusalem, and the world has got rid of its moral responsibilities for the concentration camps by agreeing to the existence of a Jewish nation. History is punishing me again. I have always believed that the Jews should be a wandering people, who meekly adapted to other nations; and now I see a Jewish nation rise. Now there is a nation to which I, as a Jew, belong rightfully and where perhaps I should go and live.

Coming out of the Bristol and then as I crossed the garden of the Tuileries, I felt inside me a boundless malaise. I feel as if I were no one, only an ugly body that doesn't know where to find refuge anymore. Céleste, Luis and Argentina, return to Italy, go to Israel, escape to the Soviet Union, to Spain? I have reached the point where I wish death would take me, the point where everything is spinning around me and I feel impotent, unable to grab even one thing.

I see the Louvre appear before me, great and majestic, and to me it seems, as to Dante's Ulysses, the mountain of Purgatory against which I would like a whirlwind to fling me. Such miracles don't happen. I seem no longer capable of going on living; too many lacerations; I feel about to explode. Perhaps the only thing left for me is to kill myself.

Dragging myself into a public room in the Hôtel Regina, I ordered a double cognac and asked for some writing paper. Then I wrote:

Dear Céleste,

I don't know if we will see each other again. We are separated only by the garden of the Tuileries and a few streets, but everything is sending me away from you, because I don't believe I can give you the existence you are looking for. I don't know what I am looking for; too many things are piling up inside me. I no longer feel my place in this world. Where to go?

I believe my life has no meaning; you can't believe I'm a Communist, and I'm not. Today I heard some terrible news: they have founded a Jewish state, with Jerusalem as its capital. I would like to go back to Italy, but under what name? Luis wants to drag me to Argentina. I would like to go on living in the hotel in rue de Tournon and talking with Recanati. He may be mediocre as a painter, even as a man, but it is rare to find someone so friendly and sincere. I don't believe I could lead a brilliant life with you in this city, which, after the war, has so changed. There are even moments when I think of betraying everyone and taking refuge in the Soviet Union. I realize this is a letter I shouldn't write you, because no man is entitled to sink to this. And yet, unfortunately, it happens. It happens that slowly wounds, large and small, mistakes, misunderstandings, historical errors pile up and lead us toward a terrible, almost unbearable inner malaise.

I am grateful to you for having loved me and devoted so much time to me. You, beautiful and brilliant as you are, don't deserve to spoil your life with a man like me, ugly and of no importance. I look at myself in one of the mirrors on the walls of this sitting room, and I see a toad. I am surely a monster, an ignoble being put on this earth by mistake, in order to cause suffering to himself and others.

I think of you, my beautiful blue angel, you who despise the Spanish world because it's too harsh

and bloodthirsty, and yet the other night you
danced the tango so well.

In this letter, my last, I have to confess to you
that during the war, in Turin, I developed a
strange physical passion for young workers,
who come home with the smell of grease
and factory on their bodies.

Their dirty hands reassure me, make me feel at
ease. In the desperation of this recent period I
have imagined how soothing it would be to
work in a factory in the Ukraine. Think: to be
nobody, lost in an immense empire. Of course,
looking out the window at place des Pyramides
and seeing the Tuileries and rue de Rivoli, I find
Paris magnificent and I think how I would have
preferred to be Chopin and not Luigi Podda.

I could also leave for Israel. According to what
I've read, there you change your name anyway;
they give you an Israeli name. I could be a pioneer, go back to making war. Can you see me
fighting on the Syrian or the Egyptian border,
me, the veteran of Caporetto and Vittorio Veneto? And besides, who would hire me? I am
dead and buried, as one of the many Italian victims of the barbaric anti-Semitism of the Nazis
and Fascists. My angel, of whom I am unworthy, what will become of me? I don't even know
how to kill myself, I don't even have with me
my old ordnance pistol. Perhaps I will take an
overdose of morphine. That might be an idea.
Dear Céleste, as you see, I remain contemptible
and cowardly to the end.

I am going to the Lotti for some morphine. The one thing I don't ask of you is forgiveness, because I know I have no right to it.

Your Tullio-Luigi

26

I come down from the garret in piazza Carignano, overwhelmed by a boundless malaise, much like Tullio's. I turn
into the arcades of piazza Castello and of via Po, walking
as if I were in a hurry, a hurry that burns inside me. I feel
ill because I no longer know what I've written, what Tullio's letter to Céleste means. Does it mean that he kills
himself with an overdose of morphine? Why doesn't Tullio
go on living, and move to Argentina? Why don't I send
him to Franco's Spain? Why doesn't he return to Turin
and look up Antonio? Why doesn't he construct a grand
bourgeois life for himself in Paris, marrying Céleste? Why
doesn't he renew his relations with the Löwenthals? He's
escaped my control! All he had to do was read in the papers
the news of the foundation of Israel, and he was off on a
mindless stroll, like the walk I am taking now; then he
stops, enters a hotel, writes a letter, and goes off to kill
himself. I could also have him not kill himself, not write
the letter. I could redo the last chapters. Is it right for him
to find Céleste again? Perhaps the mention of Spain and
the corrida should be revised, written better, described
more fully. Perhaps the San Sebastian bit is superfluous.
And what about Recanati? Both Recanati and De Feo are

mature men, real men, who know how to lead their lives coherently, and I have only sketched them in, as necessary projections of the mounting frenzy of Podda-Treves. But if it hadn't been for Tullio Treves in any case I would never have written the diary-novel. Now I am in piazza Vittorio. I'll pick up Thüsis at her school. I must read her what I've written; I feel that I, too, am becoming lost.

As we go to the pizzeria to eat, Thüsis talks to me about ballet, about Tanya, and other things; I don't listen. For some unknown reason, when we have sat down, I ask her: "Saturday would you come to the Egyptian Museum with me?"

"All right. But then I want to go to the mountains. I want to spend two days in the mountains."

"We could go on the motorcycle."

"But don't you think we'd be cold?"

We ate two pizzas and drank some Chianti; then we went back to piazza Carignano and there I asked her if I could read her what I'd written. Thüsis listened to me carefully and smoked one cigarette after another. At the end I looked at her; I wanted to understand from the first expression in her eyes what she really thought. Then I asked her: "It's awful?"

"No, it's beautiful. You know that very well, and don't expect me to start flattering you."

"How far have I got?"

"You've finished the novel!"

"Like that? With that letter, with Tullio killing himself? Don't you think it could be longer? Shouldn't I have described certain characters better?"

"But it's a novel!"

"Don't you think the letter could be an expedient, because I wanted to end the novel and get it over with? I wouldn't want to be lazy. And does this ending seem plausible to you?"

"Why? What end would you want?"

"Do you think he had really reached such a degree of desperation that he would want to kill himself?"

"If the novel ends with the letter, it's a true ending, because it leaves all the doubts to the reader. No one will ever know if Tullio went and took an overdose of morphine or whether he went instead to have an ice cream, to look at pictures at the Louvre, to visit Titina, or to take Céleste out to dinner, after he had torn up the letter."

Conclusion

In the novel Tullio Treves becomes Marcello Foa and Céleste becomes Cécile; the Löwenthals become the Blums;
Signorina Moscati, Signorina Spizzichino; Morpurgo the
lawyer, Ferrara the lawyer; Rapachi, Viano. In real life
Thüsis and Alberto Claudio love each other very much,
and Cinderella fades into a dim memory.

Paris, 1984